GREED

L. RON HUBBARD

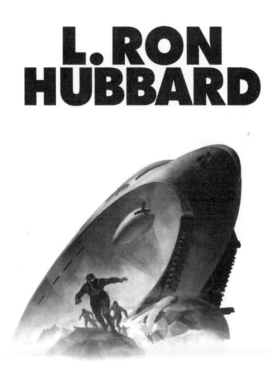

GREED

GALAXY
PRESS

Published by
Galaxy Press, LLC
7051 Hollywood Boulevard, Suite 200
Hollywood, CA 90028

Printed in the United States of America.

ISBN-10 1-59212-369-4
ISBN-13 978-1-59212-369-8

Library of Congress Control Number: 2007927677

CONTENTS

STORIES FROM PULP FICTION'S GOLDEN AGE

A ND it *was* a golden age.

The 1930s and 1940s were a vibrant, seminal time for a gigantic audience of eager readers, probably the largest per capita audience of readers in American history. The magazine racks were chock-full of publications with ragged trims, garish cover art, cheap brown pulp paper, low cover prices—and the most excitement you could hold in your hands.

"Pulp" magazines, named for their rough-cut, pulpwood paper, were a vehicle for more amazing tales than Scheherazade could have told in a million and one nights. Set apart from higher-class "slick" magazines, printed on fancy glossy paper with quality artwork and superior production values, the pulps were for the "rest of us," adventure story after adventure story for people who liked to *read.* Pulp fiction authors were no-holds-barred entertainers—real storytellers. They were more interested in a thrilling plot twist, a horrific villain or a white-knuckle adventure than they were in lavish prose or convoluted metaphors.

The sheer volume of tales released during this wondrous golden age remains unmatched in any other period of literary history—hundreds of thousands of published stories in over nine hundred different magazines. Some titles lasted only an issue or two; many magazines succumbed to paper shortages during World War II, while others endured for decades yet. Pulp fiction remains as a treasure trove of stories you can read, stories you can love, stories you can remember. The stories were driven by plot and character, with grand heroes, terrible villains, beautiful damsels (often in distress), diabolical plots, amazing places, breathless romances. The readers wanted to be taken beyond the mundane, to live adventures far removed from their ordinary lives—and the pulps rarely failed to deliver.

In that regard, pulp fiction stands in the tradition of all memorable literature. For as history has shown, good stories are much more than fancy prose. William Shakespeare, Charles Dickens, Jules Verne, Alexandre Dumas—many of the greatest literary figures wrote their fiction for the readers, not simply literary colleagues and academic admirers. And writers for pulp magazines were no exception. These publications reached an audience that dwarfed the circulations of today's short story magazines. Issues of the pulps were scooped up and read by over thirty million avid readers each month.

Because pulp fiction writers were often paid no more than a cent a word, they had to become prolific or starve. They also had to write aggressively. As Richard Kyle, publisher and editor of *Argosy*, the first and most long-lived of the pulps, so pointedly explained: "The pulp magazine writers, the best of them, worked for markets that did not write for critics or attempt to satisfy timid advertisers. Not having to answer to anyone other than their readers, they wrote about human beings on the edges of the unknown, in those new lands the future would explore. They wrote for what we would become, not for what we had already been."

Some of the more lasting names that graced the pulps include H. P. Lovecraft, Edgar Rice Burroughs, Robert E. Howard, Max Brand, Louis L'Amour, Elmore Leonard, Dashiell Hammett, Raymond Chandler, Erle Stanley Gardner, John D. MacDonald, Ray Bradbury, Isaac Asimov, Robert Heinlein—and, of course, L. Ron Hubbard.

In a word, he was among the most prolific and popular writers of the era. He was also the most enduring—hence this series—and certainly among the most legendary. It all began only months after he first tried his hand at fiction, with L. Ron Hubbard tales appearing in *Thrilling Adventures, Argosy, Five-Novels Monthly, Detective Fiction Weekly, Top-Notch, Texas Ranger, War Birds, Western Stories,* even *Romantic Range*. He could write on any subject, in any genre, from jungle explorers to deep-sea divers, from G-men and gangsters, cowboys and flying aces to mountain climbers, hard-boiled detectives and spies. But he really began to shine when he turned his talent to science fiction and fantasy of which he authored nearly fifty novels or novelettes to forever change the shape of those genres.

Following in the tradition of such famed authors as Herman Melville, Mark Twain, Jack London and Ernest Hemingway, Ron Hubbard actually lived adventures that his own characters would have admired—as an ethnologist among primitive tribes, as prospector and engineer in hostile climes, as a captain of vessels on four oceans. He even wrote a series of articles for *Argosy,* called "Hell Job," in which he lived and told of the most dangerous professions a man could put his hand to.

Finally, and just for good measure, he was also an accomplished photographer, artist, filmmaker, musician and educator. But he was first and foremost a *writer,* and that's the L. Ron Hubbard we come to know through the pages of this volume.

This library of Stories from the Golden Age presents the best of L. Ron Hubbard's fiction from the heyday of storytelling, the Golden Age of the pulp magazines. In these eighty volumes, readers are treated to a full banquet of 153 stories, a kaleidoscope of tales representing every imaginable genre: science fiction, fantasy, western, mystery, thriller, horror, even romance—action of all kinds and in all places.

Because the pulps themselves were printed on such inexpensive paper with high acid content, issues were not meant to endure. As the years go by, the original issues of every pulp from *Argosy* through *Zeppelin Stories* continue crumbling into brittle, brown dust. This library preserves the L. Ron Hubbard tales from that era, presented with a distinctive look that brings back the nostalgic flavor of those times.

L. Ron Hubbard's Stories from the Golden Age has something for every taste, every reader. These tales will return you to a time when fiction was good clean entertainment and the most fun a kid could have on a rainy afternoon or the best thing an adult could enjoy after a long day at work.

Pick up a volume, and remember what reading is supposed to be all about. Remember curling up with a *great story.*

—Kevin J. Anderson

KEVIN J. ANDERSON *is the author of more than ninety critically acclaimed works of speculative fiction, including* The Saga of Seven Suns, *the continuation of the Dune Chronicles with Brian Herbert, and his* New York Times *bestselling novelization of L. Ron Hubbard's* Ai! Pedrito!

GREED

GREED

IT can be said with more than a little truth that a society is lost when it loses its greed, for without hunger as a whip—for power, money or fame—man sinks into a blind sloth and, contented or not, is gone.

There were three distinct classes of men who made up the early vanguard into space—and they were all greedy.

First were the explorers, the keen-eyed, eager and dauntless few who wrenched knowledge from the dark and unwilling depths of the universe.

Next were the rangers, called variously the "space tramps," "space nuts" and "star hobos," who wandered aimlessly, looking, prospecting, seeing what was to be seen and wandering on.

And last were the exploiters, the hardheaded, quick-eyed and dangerous few who accomplished, according to a standard and learned work of the times, the "rape of space."

Each had his hunger. The explorer wanted knowledge and fame and he often laid down his life in an effort to attain them. The space tramp wanted novelty, change, adventure and sojourns in the exotic humanoid societies or solitudes in the wastes. The exploiter wanted gems and gold.

Hard words have been used against these last and it has been charged that their depredations in the first days of conquest committed ravages upon new planets which hundreds of generations could not repair.

George Marquis Lorrilard, sometime lieutenant in the United Continents Space Navy—that pitiful handful of space guards—was an exploiter. The savage libels leveled at him in his days are leveled even now. In the kindest histories, he is "not quite nice." And yet this man broke an impasse of Earth nations which threatened the future of all space conquest and planted the first successful colony in the stars.

He wanted wealth and he made no secret of it. A lean, hardy, ice-eyed man, Lorrilard knew his own desires and he attained them. Lesser men were afraid of him and yet, when one reviews the evidence, he never gave his own kind reason.

Often savage, always decisive and abrupt, George Marquis Lorrilard looms like a giant among his kind. He attained his goals. His fortune, wrested from brutal and inhospitable worlds, at one time amounted to twice the entire national debt of the United Continents and when it was at last dispersed in the reading of his will, it nearly wrecked Earth's economy.

But if one seeks to envision him as a palm-rubbing skinflint, cowering behind underlings, one is wrong. Even if that is the impression vengeful historians seek to give, nothing could be further from truth. He commanded his own ships. He fought his own fights. And he died in the act of personal conquest in the stars.

Not too long after exploration had begun in earnest, men found that there was wealth to be had amongst the alien worlds. All they saw, then, was the portable wealth, the fabulous jewels and precious metals and elements, which lay either already mined in the hands of hapless humanoids or was to be had by the merest skimming of the virgin ground. Some of the tales told in these times are not exaggerations. It is actually true that there was an entire mountain of solid gold on Durak and that there was a ruby measuring eighty feet in diameter on Psycho. The humanoids of Darwin of Mizar used solid silver for paving. And into a thousand worlds went the exploiters, close behind the explorers, to extract their due with pick and gun. They fought animals, humanoids, men and absolute zero—some died and some received their pay.

Few had thought of colonies at this time. Overpopulation on Earth was serious, but the first efforts with Mars had proven so pale that thoughts of new human worlds were few. Earth, as always, was too engrossed in her own travails to think much, as an entire society, about the stars.

An invention had disrupted affairs entirely. And it was a sudden and stopping thing. Heretofore, nearly all research had aided space conquest but now, abruptly, the problems of the universe had to wait. The Asian government had triumphed.

For many a long year there had been a single Earth, all properly patrolled and controlled by a single government. And the researches had become private affairs. Long sleep had lulled the salons, and the armor of their army and navy was almost sunk to rust. In the last year before the political cataclysm, the total United Nations appropriation for defense was less than one-tenth its expenditure for education, a thing which, while pretty, is not practical. And for a long, long while, the Asiatic races had slept.

Earth had, as we all know, several human races. But her most energetic were the Oriental and the Occidental. And the Occidental ruled and the Oriental endured. A country which had been called Russia had almost triumphed once. And then it had failed. Although ostensibly white, it was actually Oriental. Sunk into what it considered a trying servitude to the Occidental races, Asia struggled behind her hands and at length, with the One-Earth government grown feeble, struck with suddenness.

The wounds of a forgotten war had festered into a new invention. It was privately done. And it outstripped all the means of offense which could be employed against it.

It was a simple contrivance. We would call it very elementary now. But to Earth it came as a stunning reversal of affairs. It was a "cohesion projector." By using the force which keeps electrons and atoms together, rather than the force which blows them apart, space itself could be made into a solid wall. In an instant then, from a single generator, a column several hundred feet in diameter could be projected upwards for several thousand miles. It was not an elementary force screen such as those in early use to repel missile rockets. It was a solid, if invisible, wall. With a slightly greater frequency, it could have made matter, but they did not know that then and, indeed, did not find it out for another five hundred years.

With cunning handicraft, the Asian races, under the

direction of the ex-federation of Russia, constructed their thousands of generators, passed them secretly to proper points for installation and suddenly announced, with the murder of all the United Nations garrisons within the boundaries of Asia, that they were free from the remainder of the world.

A dozen violent attacks against the rebels ended in defeat for the United Nations. The remaining political entities outside this barrier formed the United Continents under the direction of a major country in North America.

At first no one supposed that any great harm would come of this. The Asians knew better than to attack such excellent missile weapons as the United Continents had, and the United Continents had learned with cost not to attack the cohesion barriers of the Asians. Earth was in a fine state of deadlock and consequent intrigue, and stayed that way for many years.

It was into this strange situation that George Marquis Lorrilard was born. He went to the United Continents Naval Academy, was graduated in the center of his class, was given a minor warship assignment and was forgotten about as a cog in the machinery of government. In due time, unnoticed in general but always admired by his divisions for his athletic skill and competence, he became a lieutenant and was placed in command of an outer-space patrol vessel, the *State Sahara*.

Only then did he astonish anyone. He attacked the Asian cruiser *Changrin* in the area of Betelgeuse and shot it to such small bits that he experienced trouble afterwards finding out its right name.

Returning to Earth, he reported with aplomb the

circumstances of the engagement. The United Continents and the Asians had not been at war for a decade. They had pursued their way in space without a clash because there was, after all, a lot of space. There had been tales brought back from time to time of white prospectors being robbed and murdered by Asian military units or vessels, but no action had been taken. The general idea was that any man fool enough to cruise space for any purpose did so at his own risk.

George Marquis Lorrilard not only reported—he gave forth a new doctrine, "The Freedom of Space." Heretofore there had been spheres of activity. There were no colonies as such; there were only isolated mines and occasional garrisons and patrols to keep the humanoids in hand.

George Marquis Lorrilard brought to an astonished world some news. The mortality of mines in the strange worlds was not coincident with the risings of humanoids or the happening of cataclysms. The loss of small freighters was only rarely due to collision and mechanical failure. The Asians were establishing fortresses on most of the habitable worlds in easy cruise from Earth and they would soon control space.

People had said it before. But there had not been a bloody fight involved. Lorrilard made front page with his own personal story, "HOW THE *CHANGRIN* WAS BEATEN."

It was an engaging tale. The *State Sahara*, a moldy old cruise vessel, had come upon the *Changrin* in the act of blowing the Gay Mistake Mining Company of Detroit off the face of New Kansas. The *Changrin* had landed to scoop up a few tons of bar iridium and had barely got into the sky again when the *State Sahara* struck.

It was one of those single-ship duels which were so dear to everyone's patriotic heart before big fleet battles usurped the glory of single action. The *Changrin*, being ten times the weight of the *State Sahara* and with a million foot-pounds a second more firepower, had almost won. And then, with his last erg of charge in the gun condensers, Lorrilard had nailed the enemy through and through.

For two or three days it looked like a war with the Asians, but at length everyone decided not to risk it. Lorrilard became excited and said that white superiority in space was glimmering and almost gone and that his government was stupid. They *let* him resign from the Navy.

The Gay Mistake Mining Company of Detroit suddenly presented him with half the iridium he had recovered for them. The Hot Boy Exploit Company, which owned gem deposits on thirty worlds, gave him a check for five million dollars. The August Tart Interests handed him a medal which turned out to be worth twenty millions, being a pie-plate diamond from one of their space mines. And George Marquis Lorrilard presented a very innocent face to an astonished political front. He had not solicited anything or proposed anything—he said.

But in a letter to Jacob Unser, a man much interested in the destiny of white men in the universe and a later partner in crime, Lorrilard said, "I consider that forts are a sort of trap. However, all we can do is place a new Earth out there for a base and operate from it to defend. We cannot afford a patrol navy. We need a raiding base."

Evidently he tried it. There are no records in existence

which give any kind of picture of what they did attempt. But there are a few hints.

Lorrilard seems to have tried an inferior sort of cohesion barrier, lacking the answer to an Asian type. And behind its supposed safety, on a new world approximating Earth, yet nearer to wealthier planets, he tried to plant a colony which would maintain itself and support a patrol fleet.

However it was attempted, it failed. Some thirty-eight billion dollars and eighteen thousand lives were squandered in the effort to plant that colony—only to have the Asians wipe it out. This is known because a contemporary used the figures to prove that the planting of colonies in space "is folly which would be attempted only by such a hothead as Lorrilard, the cashiered naval officer."

Other brutal opinions and a government distaste for him—for the Asians could invent weapons at will now behind their barrier, and a war would be a chancy thing—drove Lorrilard back into space.

He went at it hard-eyed now, an avowed exploiter. He pretended all the swashbuckle and the dollar-conscious conversation of your true man of greed. But one wonders if he was not hiding a rather large dream.

He began to raid exposed Asian points. At least fifty other men like him were beginning to engage themselves in this sport now. And Lorrilard became famous or, as his government said, infamous. They apprehended an Asian war as a result of such raids. The Asians apparently apprehended nothing but Lorrilard and his friends. And they rapidly fortified their areas in the outer worlds.

But it seems very peculiar, if historians of the period are right, that nothing was actually done to stop this raiding. Lorrilard landed and departed within United Continent territory at will. He banked fantastic sums, wet, as the Moscow press screamed, "with Asian blood," and went forth for others.

He used up several space vessels in the next fifteen years and his losses in personnel were sometimes high. And yet his recruiting was easy indeed. He maintained at his own expense a laboratory in the Andes for research on weapons, battle methods and, fruitlessly, on cohesion.

Two other efforts were made in space to plant colonies which would act as strong points in rival to the Asians, both efforts private and both of them wiped out to a man. And although the United Continents officially shuddered on Earth, diplomatic relations with Asiana were politely maintained. No Asian army dared issue forth from that screen on Earth to attack the superior missiles and arcs of the United Continents, and no missile could penetrate Asia. And the blood continued to flow in space.

The name of George Marquis Lorrilard, as the years went on, became something that Asian mothers used to frighten their offspring into obedience, quiet or sleep. He was forty-six now, in the prime of youth in those times, a wise, cunning fighter who had risen far above mere law.

And the incident happened which brought him to Stella

and started the chain reaction which was to end the deadlock. He was primed with new theories about cohesion barriers, loaded with new weapons and hungry for new gold.

He was familiar with Stella.

It had eight continents and was two-thirds covered by salt oceans, which is an approximation of Earth.

In age it had passed through its great mammal period and was entered upon man.

Yes; Man.

Not Homo sapiens, of course, but a very near approach, differing mainly in that he was blue. This humanoid had developed fire weapons, could work rudimentary electricity, had flight of a sort and built cities of considerable extent. He stood about two and a half meters tall, had a brain capacity of a comparative nature to pre-space man and was developed culturally into political entities.

His planet was amusing to rovers and of no value to exploiters. It was almost entirely lacking in precious metals and stones and in radioactive fuels. Therefore, it had been written up as something intriguing for the Sunday papers and otherwise left alone. Many space tramps harbored there, but inbreeding was eugenically impossible and the race stayed the way it was.

Probably colonization would have continued an entire fiasco for the next ten thousand years if it had not been for Stella.

Occasional Asian raids were made on the place to gather slave labor, but the undertaking was dangerous, no matter the value of these creatures to the Asians in extorting minerals from the infinity of worlds. The Asians, therefore, established a sort of super-state on Stella, not interfering with its politics but supporting several fortresses keyed by a main stronghold on a central continent.

Asian mine ships began to harbor there and build up financial reserves which it would be necessary to report to Asiana, and the Asian governor, a man named Kolchein, grew quite sleek. But he erred in setting up a cohesion barrier much larger than he needed and wider than any raider would suspect.

The *Sudden Sunday,* one of the exploiters, ran into this screen at an altitude of two hundred miles, tripped and crashed. As its mission was the peaceful one of landing to repair a depleted crew with Stellan converts, Lorrilard considered it a hostile act.

Perhaps he had never forgiven the Asians for certain actions they had taken against him while he was taking actions against them. Perhaps he was vengeful on account of Peter Gault, the skipper of the *Sudden Sunday* and Lorrilard's friend. Perhaps he sympathized with the relatives of the dead in the city the *Sudden Sunday* had destroyed in crashing. However that may be, it was common knowledge in those times that several hundred billions in cached Asian loot rested under the protection of Kolchein. And Lorrilard's Andes lab had lately sent him a large box.

Lorrilard, in the *Angel's Dance,* a little cruiser of nineteen hundred metric tons and armed with scarcely a foot-pound for every thousand foot-pounds in the Asian fortress, set down on Stella.

He had a bully-boy crew of two hundred, five bucko officers, and a dozen technicians. His human odds were therefore a million to one against the Stellans and a mere hundred to one against the Asians. So he sent a polite note, carried on a dagger point, to the chief mandate of the Stellan Union of Countries, and actually expected a written reply. But they did not write. A Stellan tank corps flew in at eventide and began to bang away at the *Angel's Dance*.

Some of Lorrilard's hard certitude diminished. Space tramps had been at work with know-how for a hundred years amongst the Stellans and an already considerable culture could protect itself effectively with a thing it called a "hand atomic weapon"—an obsolescence on Earth but a gruesome thing to breast nonetheless.

He lost eight men before he nailed the last remnants of the tank corps to their turrets and left them for the vultures. The attack angered him and an amazed Council of Countries dredged up the contents of their arsenals at the sight of the blue head of the tank corps commander, wrapped up in a big leaf and pinned into a package with his largest medal.

But Lorrilard was quite able. He wasn't there when the newly mustered army arrived—he was waiting a thousand miles up with his fingers on his radiative meteor disintegrators. He did not much like to do it. Things often happened which were unpleasant when the beams, usually fanned out about a ship to wipe out space dust ten thousand miles around and about, were concentrated into one package and aimed at anything as solid as Stella.

Also, it was illegal.

The Stellan army was blackening the plains below and Stellan high-altitude stratosphere battleplanes were raking back and forth in hopes. Lorrilard briefly thanked them for avoiding the Asian main fortress so wide—it was on the north central plateau of another continent—and sighed over the release button.

"I only asked them to attack the Asians with me," Lorrilard said to his chief mate, Roseca.

"Then they are more scared of the Asians," said Roseca.

"You mean the Asians," said Lorrilard, "are requiring them to fight. Well, here's for eternity!"

The button went down.

An area two hundred miles in diameter, and comprising all the plain below, smoked, bucked, buckled and caved in. An ocean of molten rocks gushed forth. The beam penetrated the crust of Stella, ate through and reached the liquid core. The guts of the planet gurgled forth. Three-quarters of a million Stellans, the pride of the race, eddied as memories in the scarlet writhe.

A lookout crisply sang: "City on two o'clock quarter."

Lorrilard looked at the city through his booster glasses, adjusted them for a smaller field and saw humanoids twisting through the streets, running raggedly and unsuccessfully between great gouts of walls coming down.

A lookout sang: "Seaport at nine o'clock. Tidal wave."

The beam penetrated the crust of Stella, ate through and reached the liquid core. The guts of the planet gurgled forth.

And Lorrilard looked down at the seaport. But he was a little late. He saw only the top of the last steeple toppling, a weather vane still staunchly pointing to a second wave coming in. Lorrilard frowned. The wave should have departed to come back in hours or days and do its engulfing. And then he knew that he had seen the crest of one begun in the vanishing of half an archipelago off the coast.

A lookout sang: "Mountains at five o'clock quarter."

And Lorrilard looked and the mountains were walking forward to meet the incoming sea and as he looked he saw a dozen cities die.

Instantly he was worried. "Roseca! Supposing the Asian fortress goes!"

And that finished the observation of this interesting phenomena, for that fortress contained several hundred billions in portable loot, small change perhaps to an exploiter if he mentioned it amongst his fellows, but not to be overlooked.

They shot away from there in a graceful swoop and approached the north continent and its plateau. And there in the early morning sunlight spread the majesty of Asiana, black-walled and grim, white-turreted and proud.

There was one wall fallen in part but every tower stood firm. The ground had moved, moved violently enough to throw a walking man heavily down and keep him there for several minutes through the successive waves. But every single ejector of the fortress was sending out screen.

"Barriers ahead," said the electrar man at his post on the bridge. He adjusted his dials and read his meters. "Altitude one-tenth of a light-year, amplitude one hundred thousand square miles. Not conning. Not conning."

"Steady on the jets," said Lorrilard. "All directors stop. All brakes back one third. All directors stop. Brakes stop. Easy two o'clock jet. Meet her. Steady on the jets. All directors ahead one. All directors stop. Stand to battle quarters! I got a new wrinkle for you, my Asian friends."

Gongs surged through the *Angel's Dance*. Roseca acknowledged stations into his phones.

"All stations manned and ready, Captain," said Roseca.

There was a lot of Navy about Lorrilard. There was a lot of Navy about the *Angel's Dance*. And small wonder—since Lorrilard was an Academy product, lost to the Navy because it didn't pay quite as well as other things, and the *Angel's Dance* had been built for the United Continents service and had been bought from the building yard when a bought senator had had a bought secretary buy her, condemning her as "unacceptable." Kolchein, down there, was finding her very unacceptable.

Kolchein was fat and Mongolian and apt to do idiotic and unprofitable things when confronted with certain semantic symbols. His fat jowls were bobbing with rage as he glared into the viewscreen in the command tower. The screen ran all around the tower as a panel of translucence, showing any visible object in its proper compass direction in any desired magnitude, and Kolchein ran all around the screen. He was looking for reinforcements. The earthquakes were unusual. They had upset him.

His cringing, whining second-in-command was also sick

from the still trembling ground, but he was more acutely aware of the value of riches and so was more pained at their threatened loss.

"It's a raid!" whimpered Sze-Quon. "It's a raid!" And he wept into a perfumed handkerchief.

"Shut up!" screamed Kolchein. "Be calm! Talk rationally!" He threw a wild hand at the image of the *Angel's Dance*. "You bag of air! You filth! You told me that our spies on Earth gave no slightest intimation of a United Continents expedition to anywhere! You told me their economy forbade long patrols this year! You said—"

"Think of all that beautiful gold!" wept Sze-Quon. "Think of my peach trees beside the gem pools in Shantung! Think of my lovely dancers with diamonds in their hair and my mansion wandering over seven sacred hills. Gone. All gone! Ohhhh!"

"Shut up!" shrilled Kolchein. "Don't weep over what you never had! Think! Think calmly! Tell me any new weapon, any scrap of data!"

"I know I never had it," sniffled Sze-Quon with all the famed stolidity of the Oriental, "but I can miss it, can't I? There are no new weapons, Mighty One. All my intelligences—"

"Then what caused those earthquakes?" cried Kolchein, adding with malice, "Dropping the gold you filch from me?"

Sze-Quon dried up a good part of his tears and took his fragile self into the antechamber where the staff were gnawing scraggly mustaches. He came back in a moment, armed with technology.

"It was a concentrated guard-fan in a bundle. We have no

concerns, Mighty One. To get close enough to touch this continent so would bring yonder vessel within our arcs." He had taken heart in the anteroom and also a small shot of *stedge,* one of the Stellan fortifiers against melancholy.

Kolchein grimaced at the screen, glaring so hard that his personality force alone should have disintegrated the visioned ship. And then, abruptly, he stopped. The vessel had changed situation in a certain, precise manner—that was his first clue. Shiphandling was a rare art when it was that good. And only one—

His fear was instantly found to be founded solidly on fact.

A vital, authoritative voice came out of the emergency-band speaker, and a face glowed above it, and the eyes in the face were hard on the screen which mirrored them.

"Kolchein! You want a continent?"

It was good, clear Asian and the only accent in it came, most likely, from a contempt for the language. And it was a good, clear viewscreen.

"Lorrilard!" said Sze-Quon. Either the *stedge* or the sight of the face revived him. "It's not a naval force! He won't blast us! It's Lorrilard and he won't blast us. You know what he wants! Gold! He won't cut this continent out from under us. He won't—" And then his jubilation changed to new tears. "He won't leave any of us alive either," he wept.

Kolchein had a suspicion of sweat on his brow. He commanded one of the strongest strong points in space. And cohesion beams were proof. He had weapons and he had numbers and he had engineers and war technicians. That was just one ship up there, the *Angel's Dance.* But it had Lorrilard.

A vital, authoritative voice came out of the emergency-band speaker, and a face glowed above it, and the eyes in the face were hard on the screen which mirrored them.

"Shut up, you vile pig!" he screamed at the weeping Sze-Quon. "You *predatil*, you *dourak*, you *soukine-sin*! Command my batteries to shoot on first range! One hundred pounds of gold to the first technician who pots that *svolotch*! Tell them!"

Sze-Quon was just fleeing from the room in a billow of veils and sleeves when Lorrilard's hard voice ate through the speaker netting.

"One thousand *tons* of gold and transport home to any *predatil* in that fort who will deliver it up to me!"

The speaker had been snagged by Lorrilard's electrar man and now worked both ways.

It was a chilly thing. It was like a purchase already within the fort. And Sze-Quon, suddenly bright-eyed, halted in his tracks and looked at Kolchein.

"A thous—" Sze-Quon checked himself, licking greedy lips. He considered himself, in the tangled politics of those times, as a member of a conquered race and entitled to a freelance hand in saving his own skin. "Mighty One! Mighty One! *Don't!*"

Kolchein's hand weapon jerked twice and Sze-Quon stood for an instant, twisting in a pillar of flames. Then there was nothing where he had been and only his handkerchief remained, still wet with his tears for a mansion on seven sacred hills.

Kolchein jerked open the antechamber door and stood glaring at his staff. He read faces well, almost as well as he shot, and what he saw now colored him violently.

"The speakers throughout spoke!" quivered a young captain of arcs. "Is it . . . was it in truth Lorrilard?"

Lorrilard, just then, was walking up and down the command deck of the *Angel's Dance*. He took a bottle from his steward, poured himself a short drink of whiskey, downed it and threw the gurgling quart to Roseca.

"All hands a drink to victory! All hands!" The cooks could be heard padding aft with buckets.

"Range?"

The electrar man looked at his captain. They made a good team when they worked this way, a team despite the fact that this was just a kid with an electronically gifted brain. Good-looking kid, too. "Eighteen thousand miles."

Lorrilard looked at the kid. "Keep them coming." He turned to his conmaster. "All directors ahead one. Hard two o'clock. Ease her. Meet her. All directors ahead two."

"Seventeen thousand. Sixteen five. Fourteen . . ." chanted the kid. The crew tensed as they swooped at the fort.

"Hard seven o'clock! All directors ahead four! Ease her. Meet her. Steady!"

"Sixteen, twenty, twenty-four. Thirty-one thousand miles. Fifty thousand miles. One hundred and ten thousand—"

"All directors back full! All directors stop."

The entire sky, at the point they had turned, went into an aching flare of light as the fort fired, twisting and snapping as great arcs sucked across the dark of space.

The crew breathed easier and grinned.

"Hard six o'clock!" said Lorrilard. "All directors ahead one."

"Ninety thousand, eighty-six . . . seventy-one . . . fifty-three thousand miles. Forty-six—"

"All directors back one. All directors stop."

"Range steady at thirty-seven thousand miles," said the kid.

Lorrilard turned to Paula, his engineer. "Character of activity of those arcs they shot back there?"

"Eighty-third degree psi," said Paula, reading her sample of contaminated space.

"Hook 'em?" said Lorrilard.

Paula had a broken nose from a brawl in some dive but she was still pretty, especially when she smiled. "Think so."

Tomlin, wavetender first, took a tube from Paula and they left the command deck.

"Now you," said Lorrilard to Gustavson, his director division chief, "tune down close on that force cone and stand by with an interlock."

"Aye, aye," said Gustavson, pushing the electrar kid aside so he could crawl into a booth, newly and economically fitted behind the range panels on this very economical command deck.

"Here we go, kid," said Lorrilard. "Keep 'em coming."

"Ready number six," said Paula from a speaker.

"Stand by, number six," said Lorrilard. "Easy two o'clock. All directors ahead one."

"Thirty-six five . . ." began the kid, chanting ranges. "Thirty-four. Thirty . . . twenty-seven . . . twenty-one . . . eighteen—"

"All directors ahead four," said Lorrilard. "Hard twelve o'clock. Hold her. Hold her. Let her come!"

The ship was staggering with this brutality. She was being turned wrong side out, pulling herself one hundred and eighty degrees off course.

"Ease her!" said Lorrilard.

"Thirteen thousand two hundred miles—" chanted the kid. "Meet her!"

The crew had seen the white and black of the fort in their gun directors and they had seen it terribly large. They were swallowing their chews and, like good space bullies, staying on target.

The *Angel's Dance* shuddered. The sky flamed blue white! "All directors ahead ten!" And, "COMMENCE FIRE!"

Paula had grappled the arcs and the *Angel's Dance* jerked like a drunk. Every plate of her bucked with the lash of her batteries.

And all down that black and awful sky ran the white-fringed fury of eighty-third psi. Backfiring. Boostered and double-ranged by riding back down the fort's own beams.

Lorrilard didn't have to look. He'd figured it out long since. He was chanting conning commands.

"All directors ahead fifty. Hard six o'clock. Ease her. Meet her. Easy nine o'clock. Meet her. Easy twelve o'clock—" She was moving very fast now.

"Six hundred thousand . . . one and one-half million . . . one and one-quarter million . . . one million—" chanted the kid.

"*Stand by, Gustavson.* All directors ahead FULL!"

There was an instant of screaming friction, a thing which rode not on sound waves nor yet existed in finite space. The grapples of the *Angel's Dance* had connected with the force cone and the speed of the intended man-o'-war, riding up now to half a light-year, tripped the formulas of velocity and mass.

There was a lurch. Men fell through the ship. The bruised steward, a girl of fourteen, hung on to the bridge ladder up which she had been coming and looked huge-eyed at her helmet, come off now with a burst strap and hanging midair in defiance of artificial gravity and all else.

Then there was a sag and an easing of the strain as though the *Angel's Dance* had pulled herself out of mud.

"All directors stop. All directors back one. Easy nine o'clock. Easy six o'clock. Let her swing. All directors back two. Meet six o'clock. Steady six o'clock. Let her swing. Meet nine o'clock. Steady as she goes!"

"One-half million. Four hundred thousand . . . one hundred thousand . . . seventy thousand—" chanted the kid. "Forty-one thousand— Gee! Gee, Captain! Look at that fort!"

People were laughing uncertainly along the battle stations. There was a buzz as arc men tried to shove the pointers away from their viewscreens and see for themselves.

And it was a sight worth seeing—to them.

The fort, the strongest Asian outpost, was in a very queer situation. It resembled a mushroom which has been pulled up by the roots and brought a quantity of dirt with it—providing mushrooms have roots that will hold.

The force screen above it, which would have conducted its batteries to distant ranges not possible at the sides and would have prevented any ship from diving at it, had worked both ways. The batteries silenced by backlash, the force screen could be hit and grappled with a snagger developed in the Andes.

But it would take a madman to hit one like that. A madman like Lorrilard. Who could lay all his money on a formula of velocity and mass and win.

Uprooted before she could disconnect, the fortress was finished and done, the whole mass of it a slab of dirt on its side.

"I wonder," said Lorrilard sympathetically, "where Kolchein vaulted up that gold."

They landed and found out.

They buried it because they could not carry any great part of it away and to this very day on New Earth, née Stella, there is a tradition of Lorrilard's treasure. But Lorrilard was much too thorough an exploiter. Before the news was out and before the technique could get old, the *Angel's Dance* laid three hundred and ninety major Asian fortresses on their sides and took their contents apart for future reference.

Probably tradition is right. Probably they did miss some. For when they came back to Earth the following year they were trimmed light for battle. They made just one attack. Moscow.

In New York, after Earth's politicos had chewed and hewed on a treaty of peace which, amongst other things, disbanded the Asiatic Federation, the Asian delegation was much horrified to know that the entire strength of the

"Grand Fleet of the United Continents" consisted of just one cruiser with a new technique and an exploiter for a captain who had no official standing.

"I say," said the secretary for defense of the United Continents, speaking to Lorrilard and, therefore, speaking with deference, "you gave us a nasty turn, you know. We couldn't find the old emergency code you used. Navy hasn't touched it for years. Thought we had an invader from space on our hands when Moscow was hit. Almost rushed aid. Joke, eh?"

"Uh-huh," said Lorrilard, looking thoughtfully at his wine.

"However, we'll repay you," said the secretary.

"You might make up for Moscow. We couldn't land for its loot," said Lorrilard. "But speaking of something serious, you know, I just had an idea."

"Yes?" very respectfully.

"Stella."

"Do I know her?"

"No, no," said Lorrilard. "It's a planet the Asians had nailed down. Earth-size. Lot of empty towns up there. Lot of machinery. Take about a hundred percent of your excess population if you'd let them go. Build a new Earth. That's it. New Earth! Not Stella. New Earth. Say, Mr. President—"

It was a king-size job, but they had a king-size man. There is no evidence to show that he ever ruled it for a single day out of time, but he has been there. He has been there for a long, long time.

If you go there, take a look at the tomb in the valley. The inscription is very thin now, just as the huge statue of him shows the wear of the ages. But it can be read. It says:

George Marquis Lorrilard
Born in Year One of New Earth
Died in Year Ninety of a
Crash Landing on Stigo

He prepared this planet,
Rid it of all Encumbrances,
Organized the first Earth Colony
And equipt it with all necessities
From his own pocket.

Ad astra per aspera

There was a verse below it, but the monument, in the course of time, has sunk so far into the ground that it can no longer be read.

Sunk even further on this site, although the fact is known to very few, are the decaying metals of a citadel and the body and bones of Kolchein and Sze-Quon.

In Lorrilard's time a large plaque was erected here, beaten from solid gold. It reflected the greatness and the coldness of the man, for it was done by his direction.

It was to Kolchein, "whose obstinance and pig-headedness made this great accomplishment possible." But somebody has long since carted it away and melted it up out of greed for the metal. Lorrilard would have understood that.

FINAL ENEMY

FINAL ENEMY

ALL these extraterrestrial races were more or less of a kind, Captain Bristol thought. They might crawl over rocks like snails or fly like birds, but their culture was definitely limited by their low intelligence. Of the fifty races so far discovered, on half a thousand explored planets, man's superiority was so strikingly manifested that an explorer was a pessimist indeed who did not expect to be welcomed as a god. The past hundred-odd years of painful and slow exploration had added much to man's knowledge. But it had not added intelligence of beings in the universe which were superior to himself.

The Aloyts were an immediate fair example. They were humanoids, with a vocabulary of around a thousand words and a culture inferior to man's Stone Age. They sat on the ground now, their greased suckerlike faces shiny in the firelight. They were decked out in childish robes. They held forth with absurd dignity on matters of no importance, which Captain Bristol and his officers of the *Argonaut VI* found boring.

Captain Bristol was a levelheaded, gray-eyed young American brought up and trained to his trade. He had seen half a hundred worlds and was not easily astonished. Therefore when Sam Catsby, whose startling facility in language qualified him as Captain Bristol's interpreter, nudged him earnestly, the captain broke from his doze expecting to find some marauding beast upon them. Hand to weapon, he glared about him, only to be nudged again, and harder.

"Captain," said Sam Catsby in a whisper, "hear that?"

"Hear what?" said Bristol irritably. "I can't understand ten words of this yammer. And I don't care to know five words of it. This planet is a dis—"

"He's saying that they've been attacked by men before! That they want to be at peace with us. That they are scared that the other race will come back and poison them again."

"What's this?" said Bristol. "On this planet?" He nudged Godolphin, his second-in-command. "Hear this, Ralph."

"From some other planet," said Sam Catsby. "He's saying that a long, long time ago, they were invaded by superior beings, smaller than us but madder."

"Oh-ho!" said Godolphin. "Been wondering how far out we'd have to go to run into this. I always said that it wasn't likely that man was the only civilized race in the universe. If—"

"Sam, get him to stop that confounded speech and answer some questions to the point. *When* was this?"

Sam Catsby stood up, his black face shining in the firelight, hand upraised courteously to halt the harangue of the Aloyt leader. That worthy stopped, leaning with impressive dignity on his tall, flower-decked cane.

"When did he see these people?" said Bristol.

Sam put the question. "He says maybe during his great-grandfather's time. That's probably about seventy-five years ago. He never saw them himself."

Bristol was tense now. This was something more important

than a planet. *If* a superior race existed—and *if* it had already conquered space—a clash was almost inevitable, should it prove that Earth's zone of influence touched on it.

Sam Catsby's questioning was long and earnest now. And the chief's replies were long and timid, as though the memory frightened him. Finally Catsby turned to the captain.

"He says they had a round ship, not like ours. Their suits weren't made of metal cloth but were like animal skins. Maybe they weren't suits at all.

"He says his own people were very numerous then and lived all over the planet. They had some cities which the jungle has covered up; and they could do a lot of things that they can't do anymore. From what I gather, he says that once they had metal knives and chest protectors. But after that invasion they couldn't make 'em anymore."

"Lost their know-how," said Godolphin.

"Go on," said Bristol, eagerly.

Catsby put several more questions to the chief and then said, "They had eyes as big as the palm of your hand, black all the way across. And each man had feelers, if you call them men. They carried little sticks and whenever they pointed them at anybody he got awfully sick. A few days later he died."

"Hand radioactive weapons," said Godolphin. "Good God, we haven't even got them yet."

"He says they were very mad. They came down outside a city and they picked up several of the people; and when some of the other people came out of the city, the invaders made a thunderstorm and it killed hundreds. He says his grandfather was part of the crowd. They rushed the invaders and drove them back to their ship. But they didn't know the importance of these little sticks."

When Catsby had questioned further he turned to the captain. "He says they cut off one member of the party by throwing stones, but the rest of them got away and took off. It must have been just a scouting expedition, because there weren't ten men in the whole outfit. This member they stoned was still alive and they dragged him up to a cave they used for their religion. They took all of his weapons away from him before he came to.

"They say that when he finally came around, thirty of them tried to hold him down and couldn't make the grade. He killed a round dozen of them and the rest got away. They barricaded the door with stones and then they spent four or five days walling it up further. But by this time a lot of them had started to get sick."

"Ask him if he knows the symptoms," said Bristol.

Catsby at length nodded and while the Aloyt waited across the fire, he relayed the information to Bristol. "He says some blotches broke out wherever the little stick had been pointed and the people just died. But they'd sent this stick around as a curiosity and everybody in all the cities on this continent had seen it. And this is the only big continent on the planet. Everybody got sick. Pretty soon there weren't enough people left to keep the jungle out of the cities. He says maybe four or five *million* people died in all."

Godolphin and Bristol looked at each other. Bristol was a little white.

They rushed the invaders and drove them back to their ship.
But they didn't know the importance of these little sticks.

As soon as he was sure that he could get no more information about the actual landing, Bristol demanded to know where the cave was that had been walled in. The old chief consulted lengthily with many people around the fire. But after half an hour, he admitted that no one present knew.

Bristol turned to Godolphin. "Ralph, take ten men and go find out what you can about that cave. Open it up if and when you find it, and give me the results. I don't think you've got much chance of finding it. Although this is a pretty slim hope, I am sending back the *Supply* to report. If we're on the rim of some other superior race, Earth may need every minute she can get. A hand radioactive weapon could knock us all apart before we had a chance to get started. And we'd find our planet in the same condition that this continent got into, with everybody dead. Go get what facts you can and meet me back at the ship when you think all chances have been exhausted for further details or when you find that cave."

Godolphin picked up his volunteers and Bristol wrote his dispatches. Before dawn the *Supply* scorched atmosphere and started on her three-month trip Earthward. There followed an uneasy and toilsome time for the expedition. Captain Bristol, with a small party, ransacked every range of hills he could find in the vicinities of the buried cities. His archaeologists were fascinated by the deterioration of culture shown by mighty walls and towers. And his botanists would have lingered over strange flora. Bristol would give them no time.

"Everything depends on the first advantage," he said. "If we can just find that being that they walled up, he may have on him some astronomical clue as to the location of his system. It has been a standing order for the last half-century to follow up any such lead as this. So far as I know, this is the first lead ever discovered. So forget about these towns." And he would turn them back to the thankless task of unwalling ancient burial caves by the score, wherein the dehydrated remains of Aloyts sat in mummified majesty. But they did not discover that will-o'-the-wisp, the invader.

At the end of six months, the *Decatur XII* of the US Navy landed at Bristol's base with urgent orders. Vice-Admiral Blanding, one of the leading space officers of Earth, inquired eagerly into the case and was even more intrigued than Bristol.

"You know what this means, Captain," said Blanding. "We've got the jump on them—or will have. The Asian findings—"

"Asian?" said Bristol. "Are the Asians around here with us?" And he scanned the landscape in perplexity.

"No, no!" said Blanding. "Exactly two weeks after we got your dispatches about your find, an Asian exploration party located on Arachne precisely the same information. The people there had been jumped and slaughtered by some strange-looking beings shortly before the aliens landed here, about seventy-five years ago. Some race, with space travel, conducted a survey into our star area about seventy-five years ago. By just plain dumb luck, Earth escaped discovery. We wouldn't have stood a chance. We've confederated with the Asians—"

"No!" said Bristol.

"It's the truth! Why, man, you don't realize! When your

report reached Earth's population, they surged around and demanded to know what was being done about it. When the Asians found what the natives said had happened on Arachne, Earth was knocked apart with riots. Plain panic!"

"But you mentioned a confederation—"

"Why, yes. Good lord, man, you've really been out of it, haven't you? And yet you started it. Well, in brief, all that would stop the riots was a terrific program of prevention. The nations of Earth formed up a central council and began to combine their know-how. Up to then nobody knew what anybody else was doing about space technique and weapons. We combined not only our science and forces, we combined our governments. We're all joined up and we're putting out an effort which would stagger you. New weapons. New research. New space navies. And all this end of the galaxy is being scanned for more news. This planet and Arachne are the only two we've found so far where the invaders landed."

"I've been doing all I could," began Bristol, defensively.

"No, no! You're important. You're more important than I. They want you back there on that council. I'm up here as your relief. They want to know everything and you're the man to tell them. We'll lick this problem, Captain, or perish trying. With a little time, we'll be able to knock any potential invader into the middle of the next galaxy before he knows what hit him. We'll even invade their home planet if we have to. And we probably should because every evidence indicates that those guys are killers! Well, now, you know the story. Get your kit and jump into the ship. I've got my hands on things here and if your entombed invader can be found, be certain we'll find him. Cheerio and *bon voyage*. You'll find a mighty changed Earth but you'll like it!"

And the admiral went swinging away to get on to his job. Bristol stood, stunned and blinking. Asia and the West confederated. All the nations of Earth in common government.

He abandoned his kit, except for a picture of his wife and the presentation sword he'd gotten when he left the academy, and swung aboard the destroyer.

"Shove off!" shouted Captain Bristol.

He had been used to the more plodding sort of vessel which had been built for capacity rather than speed and armament, and he found himself a little dazed at the way they passed comets. They retraced in twenty days what had taken him three hard months to cover the year before.

Bristol landed amid a sea of upturned white faces. Behind a motorcycle escort he was immediately taken to a meeting of the joint defense council, which had convened precipitately. Bristol was courteously given a seat at the lower end of the board and sat there blinking at beautiful uniforms and well-tailored clothes.

He was somewhat amazed to discover that he was not the first order of business. The Council of Nations which had been conducting the affairs of Earth was assembled here in force. And the first order of business was one which had evidently been left over from the previous afternoon. It had to do with the pooling of space warships.

They turned to him at last.

Captain Bristol stood, battered by the intense interest of the board.

"Gentlemen," he said, "I trust I have not sent you any capricious data. Actually my evidence is slender and our searches have revealed nothing of interest other than continued confirmation of the story all over the planet. However, some of the data I have managed to extract from the natives there—and a very suborder of humanoid they are—has been prepared into this report."

He read to them for some minutes, his voice penetrating a deeply interested silence. When he had finished he answered their questions. And then he made his final statement:

"We have very slender data here. Even this weapon they talk about is at best poorly described. But if you think the menace—"

"Captain Bristol," said the council president, "we have every reason to suppose you are on the right track. The Asian report came shortly after yours and told of similar men in similar ships who wiped out thirty-five million people on Arachne by, it seems, bacteriological warfare. In this case the invader used a spray of some sort. While no relic of the visit has yet been found, the Asians are investigating every last scrap of evidence. Additionally we have located some vague rumors on other far planets. Out there"—he swept a hand at the huge star chart on the back wall: it was studded with tiny lights which showed where exploration parties were and small flags which showed where they had been—"out there we'll get an answer. If we make a contact, we will be advised ahead of time. And we'll be armed and ready. Thank you, Captain Bristol."

In the days which followed, Bristol was in the middle of a maelstrom of activity. He found himself teamed with an Asian, Gletkin, whose experiences on behalf of the Asian government ranked him with Bristol as a fund of information.

The two of them, with a Swede named Pederson, made up a board of advice. They were whisked over the face of their world by the fastest and safest means available, giving judgment on structures, equipment, man-preservation in space and astrography.

Daily bulletins were issued over the world, giving news from various expeditions. The big star chart in the council chambers, matched in almost every home by an identical paper map, told the graphic story of search, search, search, null, null, null.

Weapon-making changed radically. Pocket flame-throwers, cuff-button bombs, two-pound cannon which would throw a million-foot-pound force behind a projectile— Military organizations died as an evolved science and became a dynamic, planned operation. And more: all the nationalities of Earth were recruited into specialized units, taught a common fighting tongue.

"Lord," said Bristol, "if this is all for naught and we never find those invaders, there isn't a political entity left that will have an independent army."

"Political entities be damned," said Gletkin. "Let's get out there and review those new oxygen bottles!"

By golly," said Bristol one day, as he and his two companions were reviewing the graduating class of the Space Academy in Paris—giving them a sweeping inspection which left many of the youngsters pale before the threat that they might not pass even after these months of training—"by golly, we've penetrated the hub of the Galaxy, Gletkin." He flipped the message in his hand just given him by a runner. "That means that we've done fifty percent of the search without result."

"Who cares how long or how far?" said Gletkin. "We'll find them!"

"They might not exist," said Bristol.

"Bah!" said Gletkin. "Young man, you look puny to me. Jump that hurdle over there fifty times. Now you, sonny—"

Day by day, week by week. And Bristol, each time he reported to the council, saw the big star map. The lights were increasing, the flags were a multitude now. On a spindle before it were dispatches which told of rich land and richer planets than Earth, strange beasts, great forests, empires.

"Captain, please appoint an expedition coordinator," said the president of the council.

"But I thought your staff—"

"No, I mean old expeditions," said the president. "There may be data from those wildcat days we can use."

It was big and hot in the council chamber. The room was packed today. Bristol got up to leave. But the great black doors opened and Commander Godolphin stood there.

He was haggard from long voyaging and he came

unsteadily across the room. He saw Bristol and brightened. Godolphin turned and motioned in another officer, an Asian, equally travel-stained.

"Gentlemen," said Bristol, standing, "I believe we have news here. My second-in-command."

Godolphin flinched at the straining necks and peering eyes. But he came forward and put an envelope in Bristol's hand. Behind him the Asian officer stood uncertainly, saw no member of his own nation that he recognized and dropped an envelope of his own before Bristol.

The captain took them, broke their seals and scanned them.

"Gentlemen," said Bristol gravely, getting to his feet again, "I have here some news of the greatest importance." He drew a breath and poured out the envelope.

Five items fell to the table from Godolphin's package. They were a pair of glare-goggles, an ancient army pistol, a rifle, a ration can and a small dog tag.

"Make your report, Commander," said Bristol.

Self-consciously, Godolphin said, "We found him at the end of a tunnel which had been closed by a landslide. He'd crawled halfway through the debris and died there, trying to get out. He was wearing an old-style cloth spacesuit and khaki and he had this stuff on him."

Bristol said, "This dog tag reads:

"TSU CHIANG-LO
TUBEMAN, FIRST CLASS
GREATER ASIAN ARMY."

Gletkin leaned over and stared at it. He blinked. "That's right! That's what it says!" And he grabbed up the Asian package.

Only three items fell out: an old space boot, a brass cartridge for a Garand rifle and an empty poison gas cylinder.

The Asian messenger looked uncomfortable as Gletkin glared at him.

"We found them in the mud," said the messenger. "They'd sunk beside the place where we figured the spaceship had landed. We panned all the dirt and got these."

Bristol looked quietly at the silent hall. He could feel the sag and sudden absence of all effort or care. He spoke slowly.

"I think, gentlemen," said Bristol, "that this is a case of cross-purposes. In the first days of exploration we were terribly suspicious of one another as nations. We never published our records or findings because our governments forbade it, trying to keep new planets to themselves. Because planets never kept the same names long and were rediscovered often and because good space navigation had not yet been invented, nobody knew where he'd been for sure. And the Asians found the remains of our expedition to what they called Arachne and we found the remains of one of their men on what we called New Chicago. The records were never properly coordinated. And so we have lost. There never was an invader."

Silence lasted long then. But suddenly the council's president stood. He looked sweepingly about the chamber and he turned and looked back at the wall.

"There never was?" he said in a challenging tone. "There never was? And we've reorganized an entire planet, entire sciences, all mankind! And we've sent our ships scurrying across hundreds of thousands of light-years to strange new lands. There never was?"

The council members looked at him. A thrill of excitement began to course through the room.

"Gentlemen!" cried the president of the council of all nations. "Gentlemen, *WE are the invaders from space!*"

THE AUTOMAGIC HORSE

The Automagic Horse

"IT ain't the principle of the thing, it's the money," said Gadget O'Dowd. "The day when I can build you a reasonable facsimile of Man o' War for ten thousand dollars, I'll know recession is here!"

Mike Doyle, the assistant chief of the Technical Division of the Property Department of United Pictures, slumped sadly behind his desk, looking at Gadget. Ordinarily they were friends but they had reached an impasse. Mike prided himself upon an ancestry which included somebody who had kissed the Blarney stone.

"Gadget," said Mike, "we pay you two thousand dollars a week to be a construction genius. Look at what you've done in the past. And now you're trying to balk at a lousy little old mechanical horse."

Gadget reached into the pocket of his ninety-dollar sport jacket, pulled out a thousand-dollar platinum cigarette case and offered Mike one of his special-made smokes. Mike refusing, Gadget lit his own with a diamond-studded lighter. He smoked pensively.

Gadget was slender, redheaded, snub-nosed and Irish. He was trying to look frank just now, but for all that, he could not quite hide a single fact about himself—he was a man who harbored an enormous secret.

51

He had been christened George Carlton O'Dowd and he had enough university degrees to comfortably paper a large office. He could have been the chief of any number of vast epoch-making research organizations but instead he was an effect specialist for United Pictures. The reason was highly classified. And it demanded money.

"This budgeteering will ruin me yet," said Gadget. "It is getting so a man can't make a dishonest dollar unless he's first cousin to the president of this company. I can't make a horse that will do what you want unless you up that budget. And that's final!"

Mike Doyle got up and sat down again on the edge of his desk. He was earnest and persuasive. "Now listen, Gadget, have a heart. I can't help what these men in the upper echelon are trying to do. They give me my assignments and tell me what I am supposed to do. And that's that. Look at the spot we are in. The script says here"—and he tapped it— "that Miss Morris has to gallop a horse out of the middle of a burning barn, bust through the doors and escape from Peter Butler who's got the place ringed with his gunmen.

"Now, Gadget, you know doggone well that the Society for the Prevention of Cruelty to Animals ain't going to let us use no live horse. This scene has gotta be big, with lots of flame, and the roof caves in immediately after the stuntman gets out of there. Now if he didn't get a chance to batter the doors down and the roof fell in and it was a live horse we was using, the SPCA would be down on us like a load of blockbusters. You just plain got to give us a decent horse. You know what happened to *Diana and the Devil*?"

"No," said Gadget, disinterestedly, "what?"

"Well, that little dog they used in there that was supposed to rescue the kid out of the duck pond up and got pneumonia and died. The SPCA got ladies' aid societies all over the country to ban that picture. It must have cost us a million and a half. Gadget, you just got to get us that horse!"

"If the Wall Street boys upstairs want to give a dog pneumonia and lose a million and a half, that's their lookout," said Gadget. "I've got to think about my overhead."

"And you got to think about your old age," said Mike. "I'll tell you what I'll do. I'm a friend of yours. I'll call up McDonnell and see if he won't stretch that budget to fifteen thousand."

Gadget waited while Mike had his secretary put through the call. McDonnell was in the studio barbershop and it took two or three minutes to reach him. Gadget fidgeted while Mike talked.

"But you know how it is," Mike was saying. "I tell you, Mr. McDonnell, even horse meat has gone up. The special-effects man is in here now and he tells me that it can't be done for a cent less than twenty thousand bucks." There were long silences interspersed with grunts from Mike. He occasionally winked at Gadget. "All right," said Mike. "If that's all you'll do, that's all you'll do. I know you got people on your neck, too. All right, Mr. McDonnell. Yes, that's the movie business. Goodbye, sir." Mike hung up and turned to Gadget.

"I got it up to eighteen thousand dollars. If you can't do it for that, we'll have to use stuntmen in a horse skin."

Gadget threw away his cigarette with sudden decision.

He was all lightness and cheer now. He had expected fifteen thousand dollars as a top figure. His head was already working with plans of what he would do to that horse. He patted Mike affectionately on the shoulder and went out. He gave the secretaries a few wicked winks as he passed them, and he started whistling the moment he was out in the sunshine.

Hands deep in his pockets, Gadget sauntered on down toward the gate. He was just veering off course to pick a carnation from the Stage Six garden for *The Buccaneer* when he heard his name excitedly called behind him.

He turned to find himself pursued by Mike. He sadly shut his mental ledgers.

"Just a minute, Gadget," said Mike, out of breath. "McDonnell must have got kicked around in the front office. He called back to say that he'd have to put an accountant on the job with you."

"An accountant!" gaped Gadget, his snub nose getting belligerent.

"I can't help it," said Mike. "Things are getting tough all over."

Gadget finally shrugged. "Well, that's the movie business. So long, Mike." And he wandered toward the gate, the carnation forgotten, gloom overcasting the sun.

Tony, his gardener-butler-chauffeur, a weasel-faced little man who played gangster parts whenever Central Casting could find him in its enormous files, popped out to open the door for him.

"What'sa matter, Gadget?" said Tony.

"We have an accountant coming up to hold a club over

our heads," gloomed Gadget. "'Don't use so much ink.' 'You've used up your allotment of screwdrivers for Tuesday,'" mimicked Gadget. "'I'm sure two drops and not three drops of machine oil would do just as well.' Blah! Movie business!"

"Things could be woise," said Tony, popping in back of the wheel and sending the Horch sports phaeton out through the gate like a lightning bolt. "I picked up two bucks on Roamin' Baby in the fifth at Santa Anita."

"Don't mention horses to me," said Gadget, and he sank down to glare at the sides of Cahuenga Pass as they ripped by.

The studio would not permit Gadget to have his laboratory on the lot since it had twice blown up, menacing, they berated him, "the lives and properties of United Pictures," to say nothing of the last blast's having knocked the toupee from a producer's head at an extremely unpropitious moment.

They had bought him a slice of Sherman Oaks on the theory that the people who lived around there didn't matter and that a range of hills between their special-effects man's dabbling and the property of United Pictures was a fine thing to have.

The Horch phaeton sliced on up Ventura Boulevard past Repulsive Pictures at Laurel Canyon and careened into the exclusive side road which led to Gadget's personal domain. When they screeched to a halt at the door, old Angus McBane, complete with blacksmith's apron, tobacco-stained walrus mustache and a paint-advertising cap, was on hand to hear the news.

McBane and Tony Marconio made up Gadget's "family." Angus was a Scotch master mechanic who had been reeducated, much against his will, by Engineer O'Dowd. In return he had done considerable educating of his own. Angus could make anything from a lady's wristwatch to an atom bomb, providing Gadget gave him the general details.

"I suppose ye've failed," said Angus.

"Nope," said Gadget, getting out and looking speculatively at his laboratory. "They upped it to eighteen thousand."

"Aye?" said Angus, hastily hiding his surprise. "But I suppose there was many a string attached to it?"

"There was," said Gadget. "We have to take on an accountant."

"An accountant!" cried Angus. "Ye mean I'll have to account for every measly wee bit of tin, and cut the corners, and save string?"

"I'm afraid so," said Gadget.

"It isna worth it, laddie. Where and away noo will we be getting the new wing for the shop?"

The three of them looked at the low rambling structure. It was painted white and had window boxes. It appeared to be as innocent as any rose-covered cottage. But this laboratory ran back into the Hollywood Hills for a good eighth of a mile. Its chambers and rooms were equipped with all manner of scientific bric-a-brac. The projected left wing was a long spur which would go underground far enough to permit an experimentation with gamma rays. It costs money to drill solid rock, particularly when it has to be reinforced against possible earthquakes. They had counted on this present job to complete the drifting.

"Let's all go in and have a drink," said Gadget. And they sadly filed into the main room which was a combination bar, museum and lounge. Tony mixed up three buttermilk flips, since the alcohol on the shelves behind was strictly for visitor consumption, by common consent.

"I know he tried," said Tony.

"Well, I didna expect any more," said Angus, wiping the buttermilk from his walrus mustache. "Noo, Chief, what onerous task begins this sad travail?"

"Well, it's got to be a horse," said Gadget. Something like inspiration came into his eyes. His stature grew. His red hair glowed. "It's got to be a horse that will run and buck and break down a door and be fairly fireproof. I think maybe you'd better start in with a hide."

He was thinking now. Like an artist who begins to conceive a great masterpiece, he forgot the financial worry and his own current project in the joy of pure creation. "I'll take care of the skeletal structure as soon as I can get to the drawing board. There's a plate of a horse skeleton around here someplace. I'll use that new alpha battery motor we built for *Frankenstein's Mate*. But the thing is, it has got to look real. It has got to act real. It's got to be a masterpiece! Angus, first thing you do is find a hide. I'll fireproof it; you just find a hide."

"Who's going to fireproof the stuntman?" said Tony.

"There isn't any SPCA for stuntmen," reproved Gadget. "Now, Angus, you get out and find me a horse."

"We canna kill it," said Angus. "There's no difference between murderin' one and burning another."

"Well, now, don't bother me with petty details," said Gadget. "I'm thinking. You just get out and find me a good horse hide—head, ears, everything. We can use that blind-man radar from *The Bat's Return* for his eyes. Now let me see . . ."

Angus hung up his leather apron behind the bar, removed his paint-advertising cap and got into an old tweed coat. "How much'll I pay, laddie?"

"Steal it if possible. When that accountant gets here we'll tell him—"

A cool voice behind them said: "You'll tell her what?"

They whirled to find themselves looking at a girl who could have been a stand-in for Hedy Lamarr. She was beautifully gowned and coiffed. She had everything about her to add charm and femininity which Hollywood could devise. But for all that, there was a grim precision which came from something unseen. It made her, as Gadget estimated in the first glance, about as lovable as one of his special effects for *The Ghost Rider*.

"I am Miss Franklin, from the front office," she said, extending her hand.

Gadget took it as though he expected it to carry thirty or forty thousand volts. "That was just a joke," he said weakly.

"I'm sure it was," said Miss Franklin. "At least I hope so. I have been looking over your budget and various expenditures, Mr. O'Dowd. The office has warned me to be very careful."

"Have some buttermilk," said Gadget hastily.

"Dishonesty," she announced, "is a thing I cannot tolerate."

"Miss," said Angus, bristling, "this lad dinna have a crooked hair on his head."

"Well," said Miss Franklin, "I shouldn't think it would be necessary for a man who already draws two thousand dollars a week."

"Miss," began Angus, ends of his mustache sticking straight up, "I—"

Whatever it was he would have said was drowned in a clank and roar from the far side of the room. Tony, behind the bar, had pressed a remote control button and now the Moloch, used in *The Lost Tribe*, with a yard of flame shooting out of his face, stepped away from the wall with a sound like scrunching bones. He reached out his arms toward Miss Franklin.

Any normal human girl, as they had many times in the past, would have fainted then and there. But not Miss Franklin. She cuffed Moloch soundly on the jaw and sat him down with a dreadful clatter of jarred parts.

"That was very effective on the screen," said Miss Franklin, "but I think it rather childish of you to keep it around. May I ask where my office is?"

Struck dumb, Gadget escorted her through a door into a chrome-and-mahogany cubicle which he usually turned over to visiting engineers. He left her to spread out her account books and pencils on the desk. He noted that she did it in a disgustingly precise manner. Now he would *never* make any progress with that "gamma room" tunnel.

Moloch, used in The Lost Tribe, *with a yard of flame
shooting out of his face, stepped away from the wall with
a sound like scrunching bones. He reached out
his arms toward Miss Franklin.*

GET 4 FREE BOOKS!

You can have the titles in the Stories from the Golden Age delivered to your door by signing up for the book club. Start today, and we'll send you **4 FREE BOOKS** (worth $39.80) as your reward.

———◆◇◆———

The collection includes 80 volumes (book or audio) by master storyteller L. Ron Hubbard in the genres of science fiction, fantasy, mystery, adventure and western, originally penned for the pulp magazines of the 1930s and '40s.

———◆◇◆———

YES! ❏

Sign me up for the Stories from the Golden Age Book Club and send me my first book for $9.95 with my **4 FREE BOOKS** (FREE shipping). I will pay only $9.95 each month for the subsequent titles in the series. Shipping is FREE and I can cancel any time I want to.

First Name _____ Middle Name _____ Last Name _____

Address _____

City _____ State _____ ZIP _____

Telephone _____ E-mail _____

Credit/Debit Card #: _____

Card ID# (last 3 or 4 digits): _____ Exp Date: _____ / _____

Date (month/day/year) _____ / _____ / _____

Signature: _____

Comments: _____

Check here ✔ to receive a FREE Stories from the Golden Age catalog
or go to: **GoldenAgeStories.com**.

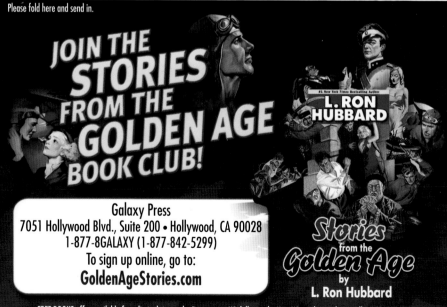

In his own office, Gadget stared unseeing at the rows of pinup girls which had been drawn especially by his muralist. He did not even notice when Tony removed his coat and slid him into his turquoise working jacket. He sank down at his drawing board and picked up his pencil.

"Well, there's other grafts," said Tony.

"Not that pay two thousand a week," said Gadget.

"Well, you don't *have* to keep on wit' the project," said Tony.

Gadget looked at him, suddenly stricken. Tony recoiled, realizing his heresy.

"I'm sorry!" said Tony. "I know what we got to do. I was just kiddin', Chief."

Gadget shafted out another glare and looked back at the board. Tony said no more about it. It was, in fact, entirely against the law to mention it around here. But all this slaving and sweating and dollar-grubbing was on the high road to as gallant and daring a project as mankind could conceive. The three of them were dedicated, soul and pocketbook, to an endeavor which would have made even Samuel Goldwyn dizzy.

They weren't going to make a supercolossal epic. They weren't going to overthrow United Pictures. They weren't going to elect a president. No, their dreams had no such finite limits.

Gadget and Company were headed for the moon!

And after that, Mars!

And after that, stars!

Real stars. Not boomp girls.

Lying in the labyrinths of this workshop, woven into every plan, staring out of each scheme, was the nose of the *Voyageur I,* a spaceship destined to make history!

No two-bit research job for Gadget like chief of Westinghouse Laboratory; no little niche like head of the Army or Navy; no peanut-sized job like the presidency of the United States or the boss of the United Nations. This Irishman had slightly larger plans. He intended to make a test voyage around the moon and then a full jaunt to Mars. Following which he was going to break the "wall of light" and get out there where they had some *man*-sized planets.

Who would trade the Earth and any job on it for the full possession of some king-sized satellites around some giant-class stars? Not Gadget. He was going to give Earth an empire that *was* an empire and become immortal in the bargain.

Every penny he could beg, chisel or even earn was tied up in the *Voyageur I.* Every one of his experiments was slanted to some improvement of that ship. Actual parts of it were scattered here and there through these laboratories, and its full design, constantly modified, was guarded by a safe in the floor so burglarproof that the FBI in full force couldn't have cracked it.

This was the secret of Gadget O'Dowd and this was the plan to which his "family" was dedicated to the death. Top secret. Top!

Tony tiptoed out of there, knowing better than to say another word. He listened at the door and after a while heard

Gadget's sixty-cent fountain pen scratching away at the horse drawings. Tony drew off.

Peeking into Miss Franklin's office he saw her sitting, making entries in her ledgers. He made a face at her back and went out to prune the orange trees. They were very special orange trees, mineralized artificially so as to produce super orange juice which, someday, would be condensed and canned for the larder of a spaceship to prevent, at one drop per day, any possible quantity of space scurvy.

A chipmunk chattered at him. Tony suddenly drew an imaginary gun from an equally imaginary shoulder holster and fired six death-dealing shots at the chipmunk.

"Take dat! And dat, you stinking swine!" said Tony. "I'll massacre— Don't shoot! Don't shoot!" But he was shot and he staggered to his knees to do a fine death scene he had witnessed in a Humphrey Bogart opus last night. Much cheered then, he got up, recovered his shears and clipped away at the twigs. He began to whistle the overture from *Aida*.

The following afternoon an incident occurred which sounded the general alarm loud enough to call both Gadget and Tony from a hasty lunch. They rushed into the first chamber of the workshop where electrical effects were ordinarily made and were startled into immobility by a very strange sight.

Miss Franklin, who, as far as Gadget could find out, had no first name, was there. She was dressed in a lovely afternoon gown with a stupefying pair of horn-rimmed glasses perched on her very smudged nose. Her pencil was poised militantly over a notebook. Facing her was Angus McBane, half covered by a horse hide which he had been in the act of dragging through the door. Angus saw with relief that reinforcements were approaching from the other entrance.

"Gadget, she's taking an inventory!" said Angus.

If he had told Gadget and Tony that Miss Franklin had been caught dismembering a newborn infant, they could not have been more shocked. Gadget glared.

"Miss Franklin, I think this is going a little too far. After all, you will find a complete inventory in my office. I am sure everything is on it which is the property of United Pictures. This distrust is heartbreaking. I cannot understand how you might suppose that we would have been so remiss as to leave important objects off that inventory. Now, these chambers are no place for a lady. That equipment you are looking at was used to furnish the dead man's scene in *The Mad Doctor*. It is rigged to jump a hundred thousand volts between those electrodes. Anyone coming in here is liable to get injured. Then how would I explain to the studio?

"I swear to you, Miss Franklin, that you will find our inventory—"

Her voice sawed into his speech like a sharpened icicle. "Mr. O'Dowd, I have already found twenty-five transformers, seventeen condensers, something which is labeled 'an alpha pile' and nine cathode-ray tubes which do not occur on that so-called inventory of yours. I suppose you can account for those satisfactorily?"

Gadget rallied. "They are my own equipment which I have

loaned free of charge to United Pictures. I have not said one word—"

"Mr. O'Dowd, you know very well that we have rules against private property in a studio technical laboratory. It must be registered with the studio. How else could one keep these matters straight? If you have been so slack in registering your own property and accounting for how you came by it, I cannot help but suppose that there are other irregularities. I am afraid that I must conduct an entire inventory of everything here."

Gadget looked as though he were on the verge of a ZaSu Pitts swoon.

"And how aboot my ain tools?" said Angus. "I couldna work wi'out them. And they are so numerous that 'twould take weeks just to list them."

"I suppose you want me to list my driving gloves, too," said Tony acidly. "See here, Boss. You want I should rub dis dame out?"

Miss Franklin looked coolly at Gadget's man. "Corn," she said. "Pure corn. No wonder you aren't even a bit player anymore. For your information, your driving gloves *should* be registered. According to paragraph three of section five of the accountancy regulations, *everything* which is used in the execution of studio business is either the property of the studio or must be registered with it for proper rental fees."

Gadget instantly brightened. "Well, then, Miss Franklin, I fear we shall have to stop work on this horse long enough to carry out the inventory which you will require."

"On the contrary, Mr. O'Dowd, I do not think that will be necessary. I have here a breakdown of past budgets. Checking back to the inventory I find that there are many items included in past budgets which do not appear on the inventory. I would suggest that you get on with your horse. I shall continue the business of protecting United's property. If there is any discrepancy, you can take it up with me later."

Gadget leaned his head up against the door jamb and beat a futile fist against the wall. "Give 'em control of money and you make czars out of 'em. No wonder the Russians revolted." He faced her again and put out a beseeching hand. "Miss Franklin, I am a scientist. You are an accountant. You are an expert in such matters. How could I help it if I made a few mistakes here and there? You—"

"A hundred and fifty thousand dollars is a lot of mistakes," said Miss Franklin. "But go on with your work. I am sure that after proper adjustment is made on these books, no word of it will reach the studio. But you have equipment here which should be sold and it is up to me to take care of that."

"Over my dead body," cried Angus. He threw down the horse hide. "Lady or no lady, I—"

Gadget quickly stepped forward and slipped his arm through Miss Franklin's. "Let's go into the outer office," he said smoothly, "and talk this thing over quietly."

Miss Franklin wavered and then reached out her hand for the bill which Angus had been gripping. "I suppose that's the bill for the thing you are carrying?" said Miss Franklin.

Angus surrendered it. And Gadget was able to lead the militant accountant into the main room. He was trying to distract her attention, but she read the bill anyway.

"My," she said, "that's a little bit high for a horse hide, twenty-eight hundred dollars. And he has even added taxi fare."

Gadget looked at it, puckering his brow. "Why, see here, he couldn't have a horse killed for the purpose. The only thing he could do was to get a stuffed horse out of the museum. That's natural now, isn't it? See? It says right here at the top, 'The Santa Ana Museum, stuffed relic of Stardust sired by Man o' War.' You remember Stardust. She was a famous racer. Now you wouldn't expect to buy *her* for a measly twenty-eight hundred dollars, would you? She won a hundred and ninety thousand dollars in just one season. And," he added with some satisfaction, "after she goes through that fire, I'm afraid her hide won't be worth very much."

"Well—" said Miss Franklin, doubtfully, "I am not interested in the cost of individual items but only in the entire budget. I have no wish to obstruct your work, Mr. O'Dowd. I am afraid, however, that I shall have to pursue that inventory."

"Please," said Gadget, "let it go until a time when I can help you with it. Many of the items you will find are alive and dangerous. Why, just last week we had a truck driver executed by a short circuit in a dinosaur from *Cave Man*." He got her back to his office and was shortly able to rejoin Angus.

Gadget picked up the horse hide.

"Why, it does look like Stardust," said Tony.

"Sure, and it is," said Angus. "Me and the curator was

howlin' savage drunk half of the night. Somehow, in the scuffle, Stardust came oot at the seams."

"What will happen to the voucher?" said O'Dowd.

"Whin the studio pays it, the curator will pay us back all but the ten percent that's to be his squeeze. After all, this is Hollywood."

"Movie business," said Tony with a sage nod. He followed his two conspirators into the blacksmith's shop where Gadget had already sketched out on the wall the structural devices necessary for the skeleton. Angus resumed his apron and blew up the forge so hot that his testing spit sizzled into steam a foot before it touched the fire. He picked up a bar of fine manganese steel, glanced at the skeleton, and began to bend it.

"'Tis a weary time that we'll have with that lassie," said Angus. "Twa nights ago, when I saw the moon, 'twas through trees, and it boded no good."

The place was soon a roaring, smoking mass of sparks and clangs. The automagic horse named Stardust was beginning to take form.

During the ensuing six weeks Gadget O'Dowd was so busy that he had little if any time to devote to his gravity repulsor. The three test units of this machine and the parts of the main construction lay deep in a hidden and so far uninventoried recess of the laboratory.

Miss Franklin was kept busy paying a stream of engineers and delivery boys from RCA, General Electric and Bell Telephone who brought odds and ends of electronic gear, looked happily at the steed, made suggestions, and went on their way. Every tube, booster and transformer was carefully recorded in Miss Franklin's black book. Meanwhile, she went on about her inventory with a grim little smile. Now and then she triumphantly confronted the badgered Gadget with some new item of his perfidy.

"Now look here," Gadget said one morning when the horse was nearing completion, "you've just got to understand that you are a dame and you don't know what I need around here and what I don't."

"I have nothing to do with that," said Miss Franklin. "United Pictures doesn't care how much equipment you have so long as you are using it or intend to use it on *their* projects. Personally, it seems to me that you would be well off to get rid of a great deal of this material. It is terribly expensive and too duplicated for any real use in the future. I think I shall recommend to the front office that we hold an electronic junk sale here."

"No, no," said Gadget hastily. "When I get time I'll explain to you just why it is that we need every piece of this stuff."

"The explanation had better be good," said Miss Franklin.

"Oh, it is, it is," said Gadget. "But right now I have a horse to finish. Has that taxidermist arrived yet?"

The taxidermist had. He was consoling himself at the bar where Tony had poured him a stiff drink. Gadget took the taxidermist and the drink back into the laboratory and showed him the completed skeletal structure.

"What an odd frame," said the taxidermist. He tapped

69

it approvingly. "Limbs in proper proportion, face structure perfect, and all in position and order. My word, Mr. O'Dowd, the National Museum could use you."

"That's what I'm afraid of," said Gadget.

The taxidermist was shedding his maroon sport coat. "Stretching the hide over this shouldn't be too difficult, providing you haven't made it too large."

"Can you make skin flexible?" said Gadget. "That's the one problem that I haven't been able to lick."

"Oh, quite, certainly. I have some preservative oils here. But why should you want it flexible, Mr. O'Dowd?"

"Oh, just a whim of mine," said Gadget.

The taxidermist had picked up the skin and was again examining the skeletal structure when, for the first time, he beheld the enormous maze of batteries, relays, tubes, antennae and electrical bric-a-brac which filled in the horse's head and barrel. It had been covered with paper to keep out the dust and he had thought that it was just stuffing. But when he pulled the paper away there was the amazing mass of wires and tubes. He backed up as fast as if Frankenstein's monster had just jumped him.

"My word!" he said. "Are you sure it isn't intended to explode?"

"Not a bit of it," said Gadget. "Now let's get down to the business of skin-stretching, what?"

The taxidermist put on his saffron working coat and went solemnly to work, rehabilitating the head and hide of Stardust. Gadget puttered with the adjustment of some final sets in the interior.

The taxidermist had picked up the skin and was again examining the skeletal structure when, for the first time, he beheld the enormous maze of batteries, relays, tubes, antennae and electrical bric-a-brac which filled in the horse's head and barrel.

"Now, cover up all those seams," said Gadget, "and make sure all those joints will move without cracking the skin."

"Move?" said the taxidermist.

"Move!" said Gadget.

"Well, my word," said the taxidermist. "This is the first time I've ever had this kind of a job. Well—that's the movie business."

"Movie business," agreed Gadget, nodding. Then he shoved his head deep into the maze of guts, busily setting the remote dials.

Angus McBane came in from the forge room and put a hot rivet through the tail-moving mechanism, which completed his work. He stood back and took a big bite from a plug of Brown's Mule chewing tobacco and expectorated expertly clear across the room into the automatic-situating cuspidor they had had to build on a temporary loan of their services by United to Universal. The cuspidor located the brown projectile by means of a radar beam and rolled noisily and hastily to get under it.

The taxidermist, catching this movement out of the corner of his eye, started back and gaped at the spittoon. He rubbed suspiciously at his glasses and then hesitantly went back to work.

Angus did it a second time and the cuspidor clanged mightily to fulfill its mission. The taxidermist, this time, was alerted for it. He leaped as nervously as the spittoon.

"Whust, mon!" said Angus. "Hae ye never seen a trained goboon? Back to ye're work, mon. Ye'll take care there with whut ye're doin'. 'Tis a dangerous beastie ye're workin' upon.

One loose seam or an onnatural-fixed hair and he's like to explode with a most terrible bang!"

With this, Angus spat once more and went away to work happily upon some part of his spaceship.

Gadget finished up some of the remaining set adjustments on the control box and then, bored, wandered out to the outer office to see what Miss Franklin had been up to now. He found a brightly dressed and briefcased young man talking to the accountant. Introduction discovered him to be Mr. Jules Weinbaum, first cousin of Artemis Weinbaum, producer of *Queens in Scarlet*, the picture for which the automagic horse was intended.

Naturally, Mr. Weinbaum had insurance to sell, and naturally Miss Franklin was buying it.

"Well, it's all cared for now," said Mr. Weinbaum. "I understand that you've almost completed the property, Mr. O'Dowd. I wish you a great deal of success with it." He shook hands again, ceremoniously, and went outside.

Miss Franklin filed the policy. "Now just because it's insured," she said, "don't get careless."

With some heat, Gadget retorted, "You look after the dollars, Miss Franklin, and I'll look after the property."

"Well, now," she said, "why be angry? I am after all only trying to do my job, Mr. O'Dowd, and you will admit that your scientific absent-mindedness has caused a great deal of mix-up in these records. If I don't do my job, I'll lose it, and I need it. I need it very badly."

Gadget looked at her, feeling trapped and not knowing

why. This accountant was not content to fight with all the weapons of her profession and the artillery of the front office, she was also using a woman's tears on him. Suddenly furious, he went into the bar and poured himself fully half a quart of buttermilk.

After two days of hard work the taxidermist was at the end of his task. He was a good taxidermist, but then, the technicians of Hollywood *are* superlatively good. It occasioned no comment that the automagic horse was now Stardust indeed, in the flesh once more, unspotted by so much as a speck of museum dust. She was real down to the last hair. Stardust had a big white star on her forehead with flecks of white ranging back into the sorrel which sleekly covered the rest of her. She was indeed a very attractive horse.

Angus came in lugging a handsprayer and a bucket. They thoroughly doused her with invisible fireproofing.

"That's a good-looking filly," Gadget said to the taxidermist. "Thanks for a fine job." He went over to the control box and lifted it by its handle to a desk.

"What do you intend to do with it?" said the taxidermist. "I never mounted anything before that had to have its joints flexible."

Gadget was not paying any attention to him. He plugged in three relays, threw the switch and twisted a dial. Stardust instantly lifted up her head and let loose a shrill whinny, at the same time rearing and pawing air. She faced around and showed the taxidermist both of her front hoofs. That worthy did a back somersault, raced out the door, went past Miss Franklin and only paused long enough on the running board of his car to grab the check which she hastily brought to him. Then he was gone.

"What did you do to that man?" said Miss Franklin, thinking she heard Gadget at the door. But it was not Gadget, it was Stardust going through her first test, which was, of course, to batter down doors. The panel gave with a crash and the filly came through into the office, ducked under the front entrance and stood in the yard, rearing and plunging.

Miss Franklin lay where she had fainted until O'Dowd found her and revived her. She looked fearfully at the splinters and then into the garden where stood a statue of a horse arrested in mid-rear.

"She does look kinda real at that," said Tony in appreciation. He and Gadget and Angus had, at this moment, become extremely fond of Stardust.

"Get me a horse trailer," said Gadget, grinning. "I've got to take her out to Santa Anita for a trial."

Miss Franklin made no protest and asked no questions. She promptly got up, went over to the telephone and dialed the San Fernando Trailers and ordered a horse trailer. She looked back at the horse as she laid down the phone. Then she looked at Gadget.

"It certainly looks real," she said. "I thought it was going to tear me to pieces."

"Well, she didn't," said Gadget, sadly.

Miss Franklin tidied up her hair and smoothed out her rumpled gown. "Well, that's the movie business," she said.

Gadget looked fondly at the horse. "Yes," he said, "that's the movie business."

Tony drove the Cadillac at a fast clip towards Santa Anita. Gadget and Angus sat disconsolately in the rear seat. Behind them smoothly rolled a standard Hollywood horse trailer, satin-lined, painted a light blue to match the Cadillac, complete with visor, drinking fountain, feed box and an automatic disposal unit. It was beginning to get dark as they drove down Colorado Street in Pasadena. They were almost there.

Gadget looked at his ruby-encrusted wristwatch. "I don't understand it," he said. "Everybody can rob the studios but us." And he broke the rule which he himself had made. "It isn't as if United wouldn't get the benefit of it. Why, when those headlines hit the papers United will be in about every fourth paragraph. They couldn't buy that publicity for ninety million bucks."

"And they would'na finance it for ten measly cents," said Angus.

"Maybe we can put the squeeze on somebody," said Tony. "If kidnapin' just wasn't so illegal—"

"I don't wish Miss Franklin any hard luck," said Gadget, "but I wish she'd accidentally fall off the Colorado Street Bridge. It's going to cost us a couple of hundred thousand dollars to buy back our own equipment. And after all the trouble we had chiseling it, too."

"How much?" said Tony, shocked.

"Well, ninety thousand so far," said Gadget sadly.

"Maybe we could crack a bank," said Tony.

"Probably have to give up the whole expedition," said Angus. Instantly he was fixed with glares from both Tony and

O'Dowd. And he sank back with some self-satisfaction to gnaw off his plug of Brown's Mule. The expectoration into the windstream splattered the horse trailer.

They wheeled into the gate and made themselves known to the guard. Gadget's studio card immediately availed them of an attendant's services and dispersed the gathering dusk under an onslaught of floodlights.

They stopped the car. The track wheeled away from them in both directions. The grandstands gaped emptily above them. A few hostlers and touts were wandering around the stables in the far distance. Near at hand some belated losers still gloomed at the rail. Two other horse trailers were in sight. Gadget went beyond the starting gate so that his activities would be hidden from view.

Tony scrambled around and opened up the rear of the horse trailer. Gadget set up the control box under the rail. And Angus laid out a set of tools in case any adjustments had to be made. It was their intention to give Stardust a good, thorough test. Otherwise, they could very well hold up production on *Queens in Scarlet* for a day or two by a minor breakdown, which item would cost the studio at least a hundred thousand dollars, due to stars' salaries, stage rentals and other overhead. One lost day's work for Veronica Morris alone would be worth retiring on. Technicians have to be accurate in the movie business.

Tony set up two cases of soda and a package of sandwiches. Then he peeled off his chauffeur's coat to don the frontier buckskin jacket which the stuntman would wear in the scene when he impersonated Veronica Morris. This was strictly rococo. But, as Tony explained, "I gotta get into the mood for the part."

Stardust backed out of the trailer under her own power. She stood breathing quietly and occasionally snorting and flicking an ear, while Angus fixed the saddle on her. It was an English exercise pad about half of the size of a postage stamp. Even so, little Tony's smallness made it seem quite adequate. Tony mounted and located the stirrups with his toes. He spoke encouragingly. Stardust moved her eyes, pawed and moved off with the sideways restlessness of a racehorse.

"Pretty good, huh?" said O'Dowd. "I spent two hours last night lookin' at some films of her when she was in her prime. Now watch this."

Stardust shook her head in a huge negative, snorted and cakewalked forward.

"Say, that's pretty good," said Tony. "I remember that. By golly, you got me half tricked into believin' this *is* Stardust."

"Wul, be keerful of her, laddie," said Angus. "When she was alive she brought me nathing but travail and sorrow. I ken losing seventy-five cents on her to that scut of a bookie Finklestein."

Stardust capered and cavorted. Tony had to do a little expert riding to stay with her. But then, this was in Tony's line. In training up to be a bit player he had undertaken almost any sport you could name. He was fully as proficient on a saddle as he was in an airplane. The only thing which kept him from being a stuntman was an irrational desire to go on living in one piece.

Gadget sent the horse down to the starting gate. Without any attention from the operator Stardust was able to find a box and go into it, stopping when she approached the gate itself.

"You are not going to run her?" said Angus.

"Well, according to the script," said Gadget, "she has to do a two-hundred-yard sprint after she gets out of that broken door. It's all in one shot, to convince the customers. So she'd *better* know how to run. All right there, Tony. Are you ready?"

"Let's go," said Tony. "Shades of Man o' War. I wish this was a real race."

The floodlights glared down upon the track, the gate sprung and Stardust rushed forward, buckjumping the first six strides and then settling into a long, distance-devouring run. Tony, well into character now, laid on his quirt and yelled encouragingly into the horse's ear. Gadget gestured at the control box and Angus took over. O'Dowd jumped up on top of the Cadillac so he could see better.

Stardust went around the turn, came into the back stretch and began to thunder home. She was splitting the air like a lightning bolt. Above the pound of hoofs Tony's shrill "Git! Git! Git!" and "Hi! Hi! Hi!" resounded. Stardust came into the homestretch, speeded up and dashed across the finish line.

Gadget went down, took over the controls and brought the mount to a plunging halt. Stardust came trotting daintily back toward the parked trailer, tossing her head, jingling her bit and making snorty noises which indicated that she was out of wind.

*Stardust went around the turn, came into the back stretch
and began to thunder home. She was splitting the air
like a lightning bolt.*

"Boy, she sure can run," said Tony.

"We'll give her two more trials," said Gadget. "And then we'll go over to that old western town later tonight and batter down a couple of doors. She's got to be all ready by Wednesday."

He was about to turn a dial on the control box when he noticed three men standing at the rail, looking interestedly at the horse. He was about to ignore them when he recognized one of the men from his pictures. It was Cliff Neary, the comedian and racing dean, who squandered the millions he made acting, on horses. Beside him was his trainer and an exercise boy.

"Just watching your horse run," said Cliff. "Didn't know that Stardust had any colts." Cliff put out his hand to Gadget. "I'm the owner of the Neary Stables," he said. "This is my trainer, Hank."

"Gadget O'Dowd," said Gadget, shaking the extended skin.

"Oh, yes," said Cliff. "The special-effects man. I remember that we contracted with United for some of your work on my *Road to Smolensk*."

"*Road to Smolensk*," said Gadget thoughtfully. "Oh, yes, that was the vodka that broke into flame every time Roy Ellis spat."

"Good job," said Neary.

"There was nothing much to that. The things that were difficult in that picture didn't show at all."

"I know. You fellows never get much credit for all the little odds and ends that it takes to make a show hang together.

But what are you doing out here with a horse? I didn't know that was in your line."

"Well, she's kind of a funny horse," said Gadget.

"Mighty good-lookin' one," said the trainer, staring at Stardust hungrily.

"By the way," said Cliff, "you wouldn't like to put her up against three or four of mine, would you?" He was trying not to look sly. "Nothing like a good horse race after a long hard day's work at the studio."

Angus gaped and was on the verge of laughing when Gadget silenced him with a glare. "Well, now," said Gadget, trying not to appear eager but negligently pulling half a dozen thousand-dollar bills out of his shirt pocket, "don't mind if I do."

"'Don't mind if I do' is right," said Cliff. "Hank, bring Thunder Mountain over here. Do you think you can boot him through as a winner, Pat?"

Pat, a jockey, gave Cliff a white-toothed grin. "I reckon I can, Mr. Neary."

Tony watched all this with eyes which got wider and wider. Then he began to laugh. "Listen, pal," he said to the jockey, "this is pretty tough company you're riding in. The last three jocks that tried to beat me got buried, with horseshoes of roses. I don't beat easy, see?"

The jockey grinned and helped Hank bring Thunder Mountain up to the rail. The horse was a big, powerful stallion that Cliff had bought for quite a piece of change. He was being kept under blankets until the Neary Stables could make a cleanup with him. Thunder Mountain, Cliff fondly believed, could make Man o' War look like he was tied to a post.

Stardust breathed easily now and cavorted a trifle, edging near Thunder Mountain. That worthy, having horse sense, took one look at the bogus filly and whistled shrilly, backing off.

"Whoa now, boy," said Cliff. "I never saw you lady-shy before."

Thunder Mountain reared, shook his head angrily, and whistled again, backing even further away from Stardust. Gadget took his cue and removed his automagic horse down to the gate.

Presently they had both mounts behind the wire. And the race was ready to be run. The trainer held up a blank cartridge pistol, Angus got ready to release the gates, and Cliff eagerly yelled some final riding instructions to Pat. Gadget tried not to appear too interested in the control box on which he was sitting.

The gun roared. The gates sprang up. And horse and pseudo-horse were off in a cloud of sawdust. Gadget had to trust to it that the last running speed would at least keep in distance of Thunder Mountain until they reached the homestretch. Then he hoped he could adjust matters. The six crisp thousand-dollar bills were weighted down by a rock, in company with another half dozen just like them which were fresh from Cliff's purse.

Angus, up higher, could see better. He began to make wild signals toward Gadget, who turned up the running speed a notch.

The horse and pseudo-horse came into the backstretch with Thunder Mountain a full furlong in the lead.

The shrill "Ki yi" of Tony rose above the wheezes and grunts of the running mounts and the pounding of their hoofs. Angus was making despairing motions with his hands, and glancing sideways now and then at Gadget.

O'Dowd was not idle. He pulled up the dial and very perceptibly Stardust began to close. When they were still seventy-five yards from the finish a wide gap yet remained. Gadget upped his dial another notch. Stardust's stride lengthened. Thunder Mountain, straining and lathered, felt the pseudo-horse surge alongside. He put on another burst of speed. But he was no match for Gadget's fingers on the dial. Stardust came neck and neck with Thunder Mountain.

In a close finish there was still no argument. Stardust had won!

Cliff turned disconsolately to Hank. "I thought you said that Thunder Mountain could run," he said. "Oh, well, easy come, easy go. Mr. O'Dowd," he added with a bow, "the money is yours, suh. And it is a pleasure to lose to such a gallant gentleman."

Gadget stood looking at the fluttering green leaves. His conscience was hurting him.

"Mr. Neary," he said, "perhaps I ought to tell you that that horse of mine—"

"No, no," said Cliff, "a race is a race." He was looking at the mounts as they came up. They were blowing and whistling from their run. "Say now, that's mighty peculiar. That Stardust of yours doesn't even seem to be winded."

Gadget's heel came down on the control box. And Stardust really began to blow.

"No, he really isn't—I mean *she* really isn't," said Gadget. "In fact, I dare say, she could probably run another race if she had to."

Cliff looked up alertly. He glanced at the twelve bills and then at O'Dowd. "You don't mean to tell me that you'd be willing to risk another slight run for the money?"

"Well, now," said Gadget reluctantly, "I think I probably owe it to you, Mr. Neary. Just the same—"

"Well, say no more," said Cliff. "Hank, bring up Sassy Lassie and we'll spin her around again. That is, of course, Mr. O'Dowd, if you have no objections?" If a man wanted to run a blown horse, who was Cliff Neary to refuse the money.

Gadget didn't, and the horses were soon lined into position. Sassy Lassie turned out to be a high-strung filly that the perspiring Pat found hard to manage. She tried to climb the rail, then the starting gate, and finally consented to stay in position. Twenty-four thousand dollars, twelve of it in the form of a check on Cliff's bank, were now secured by the rock.

"We can't wait forever," said Cliff, afraid Stardust would get rested, "let 'em go."

The pistol banged, the gate lifted, and horse and reasonable-facsimile-thereof rocketed out into the track. Angus was standing high up, madly chewing Brown's Mule, and wondering about the strength of the various pins and cogs. He was wishing that he had foreseen this turn of affairs when he was at his forge.

Gadget, having surreptitiously tuned Stardust's eyes to a set distance off the rail, looked up to Angus anxiously for a signal.

Gadget's conscience was hurting him. He liked Cliff because Cliff was a swell guy. "But when he finds out what the cause is he'll laugh about it," Gadget apologized to himself. Many times before he had vowed that he would pay the studio and his victims back once the fact had been accomplished and man had made a voyage to the moon. His conscience thus assuaged, he was willing to forget it and enjoy the horse race.

Angus was making wild motions and Gadget upped the speed notch, only to find out that Angus' arm signals became wilder. Accordingly, Gadget slowly backed it down again. An action which resulted in the Scot's relaxation.

The filly and Stardust came scrambling into the stretch, pounding forward, straining every muscle and kingpin. Stardust was about eight lengths in the lead. Gadget understood his mechanic's earlier concern. Evidently the pseudo-horse had been traveling like a jet-job around the first turn. Gadget backed off the control dial even further and let Sassy Lassie catch up. They finished in a cloud of dust and hurrahs, out of which the fact dissolved that Sassy Lassie had been whipped by half a length.

After a little, Pat and Tony came back. The jockey was blowing and round-eyed.

"Mr. Neary," said Pat, "that there Stardust run away from me at the start like an airplane. I didn't think I'd ever catch up."

"It's all right, Pat," said Cliff. "Some days you can't ever see the back of your neck. Mr. O'Dowd, that's some horse you've got there. I wish there was a little more light, I'd like to look at her teeth."

"Oh, her teeth are just fine, fine," said Gadget.

"I'm serious," said Cliff. "Now probably you've got a lot of things to do besides monkey with a hobby like racehorses. Personally, it's not very lucrative. And if you are just starting out you ought to take the advice of the old master and give it up at the beginning, while you are still on the winning end. There, you're twenty-four thousand dollars richer—"

"Eighteen," said Gadget. "I've got no objection to horse racing, Mr. Neary. There are just some people who can make money out of it and some people can't. Didn't you say that you had another horse around here?"

"Well, fan my brow," said Cliff. "Don't tell me that that filly of yours can run again?"

"It's like this," said Gadget, "I've raised her up from a . . . colt. She wouldn't be nothing but skin and bones if it weren't for me. And she knows it. She appreciates a good trainer when she has one. She'd be happy to run another race. Of course, I'll admit it's kind of dark—"

"See here, now," said Cliff, "if you think you can do it without wind-breaking her, I've got Old Hundred over here. He's one of the fastest geldings I ever had in my stables. If you don't mind taking another check?"

There was a sliver of the moon showing in the west. Gadget cocked one eye at it and then looked at Cliff. "Mr. Neary, that check is good enough for me."

Old Hundred came up and went down. And when the dust had settled, Cliff stood with his hands in the pockets of his leather jacket, the brim of his hat pulled down, and his shoulders hunched with chill.

"I'm sorry, Mr. Neary," said Pat, climbing down from Old

Hundred. "When we got into the stretch I just plain couldn't even see that filly's tail. She was that far ahead. Maybe I just ain't much of a rider, Mr. Neary."

"Oh, say not so," said Cliff, putting his arm around Pat's shoulders. "You're just up against a wonder horse, that's all." He snapped his fingers, whistled and looked at Gadget. "That's three times I've been trimmed, Mr. O'Dowd. You wouldn't consider selling that horse, would you?"

With Angus and Tony looking on and gaping, O'Dowd gazed first at his toes, then at the moon, and then at Mr. Neary. Gadget knew his danger here. If he didn't go along with this sale, Cliff, horse-hungry, would become more and more insistent, finally discovering the extremely mechanical identity of Stardust—a discovery which would lead to argument.

"Well, I might entertain an option," said Gadget, "on one condition."

"Well, now, a little old thing like a condition," said Cliff, "shouldn't stand between a couple of good horse-traders."

"The condition is that she won't ever be used for breeding purposes."

"I think that could be arranged," said Cliff. He looked kind of sly and disinterested. "Would . . . er . . . fifty thousand dollars make the deal attractive? Say, ten thousand now as an option and forty thousand dollars tomorrow?"

"Oh, I can't deliver her right away," said Gadget. "She's on a special diet and I wouldn't dare take her off of it. You'd be surprised how that diet affects her. I have been making some scientific observations on her, too. And they won't be complete till Thursday morning."

Angus and Tony looked on in amazement. They had never got used to the glib and convincing way Gadget had with him when the necessity demanded it.

"Why Thursday morning?" said Cliff.

"Well, I've got to observe the final effects of this diet. And then you can have her."

"You'll give me the diet, too?"

"You bet I will," said Gadget.

Cliff finished writing out his check and gave Gadget his hand. "It's a deal, my boy. My trainer will be up at your place Thursday morning to pick up the filly. Come along, Hank, let's get out of this place while we still have enough money left to pay Uncle Sam his income tax. Goodbye, Mr. Marconio and Mr. McBane. Come on, Pat, you'll be riding winners yet."

Gadget stood looking after them as they left.

Angus grabbed his arm. "Och, laddie, how terrible it will be, the sight of you behind bars. Not only are you sellin' him somethin' that ain't a horse, but it's the property of United Pictures. Crime does not pay, me boy."

"Not very well, anyway," said Gadget, thinking of Miss Franklin. "But cheer up. We have till Thursday morning to think up the rest of the idea."

"You mean you don't know?" said Tony.

"No, not yet," said Gadget.

"What a noive," said Tony, "what a noive! Let's load up and get out of here before you have any more of these half-thought-up ideas."

"Remind me when we get home to put the entry in my book: 'Eighteen thousand dollars to be paid back with interest to Mr. Cliff Neary.' He was just too nice about it. I haven't got the heart to take the money without putting it in my book to be paid off. Even if we did win it fair and square. After all, he asked us to race, we didn't ask him," Gadget said.

"What about the option money?" Tony asked.

"Don't worry, we'll figure out something." Gadget seemed rather cheered now that he had decided to put Cliff's name in the book as one of those to be repaid when the trip was finally made. He fingered the checks and even whistled a little on the way home.

Stardust, having successfully broken down six doors without having sustained any injury, left the western set north of San Fernando in a shocking state of disrepair, and on Wednesday the shooting of the picture started on schedule.

At seven o'clock in the morning everybody bundled up and went on out to the location at Gray's Ranch. Amongst the usual horseplay between the cameramen and the assistant directors, Gadget looked over the scene of action.

A big flimsy barn had been built. The rooftree was sawed half through and when the building burned, that roof would come down, but quick. Wires and pulleys would assist the cave-in of the roof, and mounds of hay containing flares were piled all about. The property man was giving the hay a final sloshing with smudge solution. There had to be a lot of smoke.

The stuntman went over the place to make sure there was nothing to trip over. He was a devil-may-care young man to all appearances. But in common with all good stuntmen, the largest part of his daredeviltry consisted in the minuteness with which he planned the staging of his scenes. He bore several scars and had a slight limp, all of which came from some director's miscalculation in regard to falling off cliffs or leaping through plate glass windows.

The stuntman spent a few moments with Gadget going over the details of the shot.

Veronica Morris and Peter Butler were there eating a belated breakfast in the shade of Butler's dressing room trailer. Marty Fitzgibbons was regaling them with an English music-hall anecdote.

"Hello, Gadget," Mr. Butler called out. "That's Gadget O'Dowd over there," he told Miss Morris.

"Where? Oh, hello, Mr. O'Dowd. I hope you fixed it so that poor stuntman won't get hurt. I'd feel pretty dreadful if anything happened to him for my sake."

"He'll make it all right," said Gadget, accepting the leg of chicken that Mr. Butler's valet handed him.

"Let's see it," said Mr. Butler, interested and getting up.

"Now, now, folks," said the director. "There's no hurry about this. Morning, Miss Morris. I'll have a cup of that coffee if you don't mind. Well, I see that you got the horse here all right, Gadget."

"I want to see that thing in action," said Mr. Butler. "I almost died laughing over that mechanical monkey Gadget built for the last Tarzan picture."

"Oh, I remember that," said Miss Morris. "He was certainly a wonderful 'animal.' Where is it now, Mr. O'Dowd? I don't suppose you could be persuaded to part with it?"

"The last I saw of it," said Gadget, "it was jumping up and

down on Jacky Bocker's front lawn. When the accountancy department gets through with me I suppose it will be lying on the scrap-metal heap in some local junkyard."

A cameraman came up with an assistant director. "We got three cameras on it, sir."

"Well, make sure you get it the first time," said the director. "That barn will only burn once."

Gadget put down the chicken bone. "I suppose that's my cue," he said.

"I've got to see this," said Mr. Butler. He picked up his "bad man's hat" and followed O'Dowd over toward the horse trailer. Angus was ready with the control box. And Tony let down the back gate. Stardust stopped being immobile and began to champ and whinny. She backed down the ramp, turned, pricked up her ears and, at Gadget's tip-off wink to Angus, Stardust came nuzzling up to Veronica Morris for a piece of sugar.

"Why, it's a real horse," said Veronica.

"Not if you put your ear to it," said Gadget.

"Why, that's Stardust," said Mr. Butler, "that won the sweepstakes."

The director took one look and turned to the script girl. They put their heads together for a moment and the director came up. "It won't do," he said. "Two scenes further along, that we've already shot, have a sorrel without any forehead blaze."

"Sorry," said Gadget. "They didn't give me a script. Angus, hand that box of paint down here."

In a very short space of time, watercolor had remedied the

situation handsomely. And the script girl was satisfied. The property man came over and saddled Stardust with the proper riding equipment. The stuntman gave his mount wide-eyed admiration.

"Mind if I try a couple of tests on it?" he said. He mounted up. Gadget made the horse prance, cavort and strike with its front feet. Finally he put Stardust into a dashing run.

"Well, for once," said the cameraman, "we won't have to speed the film up on that one. That hunk of junk can really get out of here."

The director gave the order for "Places!" The sound man took his tests. The front doors to the barn were securely barred on the stuntman. Gadget took up his station just off scene, where he could look through a window into the barn, see the front door and the road which went off along the side of the corral. He had his control box all adjusted and tuned.

"Camera!" said the director. "Action!" An expert archer sent a blazing arrow across the scene into an explosives-loaded hay pile at the front of the barn. A second firebrand followed it, sticking in the side wall. A third thunked solidly into the shingles and in a moment the dry explosive-impregnated material flared and yellow fire curled greedily across the structure. More hay piles caught. A second stuntman ran forward. He was dressed in Huguenot garb. He pitched a torch in through the barn window.

The flames were beginning to crackle and roar. Gadget waited until the entire front of the building was blazing. Then, with an urgent wave from the assistant director, he set

Stardust in motion. The roof was already beginning to sway. The temperature in the barn must have mounted to about a hundred and thirty degrees. Stardust began to plunge and rear.

Then it dashed forward, flung up its hoofs, and brought them down solidly against the doors.

Outside, on signals, two Huguenot soldiers came up to lower arquebuses at the entrance. The doors caved. The assistant director's men gave a yank and the roof started down.

Out came Stardust! Narrowly missed by two blazing beams, nearly swallowed in clouds of white smoke and billows of yellow fire! The stuntman, dressed in lady's riding garb, was leaning on the neck and holding on in earnest. Stardust plunged, affected to rear at the two extras, who now blazed away with their two arquebuses, and fled off down the road at a fast run! Arrows and crossbow bolts thunked in her wake. She vanished far up the lane. The director called "Break!"

Next followed three shots, done on another set, of the now somewhat singed Stardust plunging and rearing in a mock interior. She had to break down a burning door in here, too. At eleven o'clock the work was finished. And, mounted on a real horse, Veronica Morris was ready to follow through with the close-ups. Mr. Butler was due to "perish" tomorrow. So today he could look on.

Gadget, having lunched with the director and chief cameraman, receiving plaudits all around for his remarkable horse, was now free to return to his laboratory and do what he considered more important work.

As Gadget and Tony were backing Stardust up to the

horse trailer, they had one slight encounter with the SPCA representative who wanted to examine the "injuries sustained by the horse in that last scene." In the end, the man, who turned out to be quite a nice fellow after all, was their most appreciative audience. He just couldn't get over it. They let him examine a couple of the bolts down the throat, and unscrew a couple of teeth. "You are a genius, my boy," he said. "You are a genius. You should have proper recognition. Why, there are museums all over the country—"

"Oh, no," Gadget said hurriedly, "I could never do it again. It was just a fluke."

They finally escaped from the terrible prospect of the very unprofitable "proper recognition." "That was a narrow one," said Gadget as the man walked away. "If we ever got 'recognition' we wouldn't make enough to fly to Canada, much less the moon."

They loaded the scorched Stardust into the trailer and they wheeled on home.

Miss Franklin was waiting for them. She had, gripped in her hand, a green slip of paper which she had obviously been holding half of the morning in anticipation of their return. Gadget took one look at it and knew what it was: the twenty-five hundred and twenty dollar kickback from the racing museum, twenty-eight hundred dollars minus ten percent.

"Now don't tell me this is a personal debt," said Miss Franklin in a silky voice. "The boy told me that he was to give it only to Gadget O'Dowd."

"Then how did you get it?" said Gadget.

Tony looked mournfully at a torn-up flower bed. "Boss, she can wrastle, too."

"That skin the racing museum gave your mechanic can go right back to them. It will cost me a whole lot less than twenty-eight hundred dollars to have it restuffed. It looks to me, Mr. O'Dowd, like you didn't need any such budget. This makes you exactly two thousand and five hundred and twenty dollars under your estimate."

Gadget looked at her and sighed deeply. He went into his own office and slammed the door.

The following morning bright and early Cliff's trainer, Hank, drove up with a horse trailer which made the rental job look like something off a salvage pile. His men opened the door of this glittering creation invitingly. Hank went into the office to find Mr. O'Dowd. Fortunately Miss Franklin considered her office hours to be from nine to five. Movie people are ordinarily up long before that.

"Well, well," said Hank, "here I am."

"Well, well," said Gadget, "I see you are."

"Shall we load the horse aboard now?"

"Well, you see," said Gadget, "I've been thinking this thing over rather carefully and I've decided—"

"You're not going to back out on the deal now!" said Hank.

"Well," said Gadget, "I was thinking—"

"Mr. O'Dowd," said Hank, "you look to me like a man of your word. You wouldn't go back on Mr. Neary, would you? He could do you a lot of good."

"That isn't all he could do to him," said Angus under his breath.

Gadget was thinking fast. If he confessed this sin he would certainly have to refund Cliff's losses. But if he didn't, then he would have to give Cliff the horse. Due to his disturbed state of mind because of the twenty-five hundred and twenty dollar hole in the budget, he had not come up with the brilliant idea of which he had thought himself capable.

"Where is the horse?" said Hank suspiciously. "She's all right, isn't she?"

Gadget was about to report the theft of Stardust when one of the men spotted her in the bar. "Funny place to keep a horse," said Hank. "I hope she doesn't drink! Well, shall we load up?"

"She looks kind of singed," said one of the men. "What happened?"

"Nothing serious," said Gadget. "Nothing serious at all."

"Funny look about that horse," said the other man.

"Well, she's just a little bit off her feed today. All that running didn't help her any. Tony, we are being very remiss in our hospitality. Take these gentlemen inside and give them something to eat or drink."

"I got a fresh cup a coffee if you want some," Tony said.

"You go ahead too, Hank. I'll put her in the trailer," Gadget said.

Tony hustled them inside, and Gadget loaded Stardust on board the super-deluxe horse trailer. When they came out again Hank saw Stardust's ears above the trailer side, handed Gadget the check from Mr. Neary and they agreed to sign all the necessary papers on Saturday morning. Hands were shaken all around and soon the yard was deserted.

Ten seconds later Miss Franklin drove on the scene.

"What was that horse trailer?" she demanded.

The smile which Gadget had worn at the departure now vanished. "Well, you see, that Stardust—"

"You mean you've let somebody else have a piece of property belonging to United Pictures? You must realize that there is a lot of valuable equipment in there that can be salvaged," said Miss Franklin primly. "You've already exceeded your—"

"D'ye mean to say that we've got to go to all the toil of taking that horse apart?" said Angus, coming belatedly to work.

"I mean just that," said Miss Franklin. "We'll restore that hide to the museum and put all the various parts on the inventory." She went into her office and could be heard arranging things for her day.

Gadget looked at Angus. "Bring the control box out," he said.

Angus was in no mood to be lightly ordered about, but he went. "Dismantlin' a horse!" he was snorting. "Filing parts! Inventory! What the movie business isna comin' to would— What in the saintly name has happened to this control box?" He came back out, his basic anger building. "Musther O'Dowd! Some scut has unsoldered—!"

"Give it here," said Gadget hastily. "I was in a hurry. I didn't know when they'd look at me. Give me that box!"

Miss Franklin, curious as to what was going on out in the court, issued from her office, aggressive as an overdue bill.

"What are you doing?" she demanded. "When the front office learns—"

Suddenly a roaring whine resounded in the sky. Looking up, a terrified Miss Franklin beheld a horse! It had been rising ever since the trailer had begun to move, having issued straight up, and now it had a very, very long way to come down.

Miss Franklin screamed! Stardust was falling faster now, falling with the gathering speed of a blockbuster, falling so fast that the air was split and scorched.

Down came Stardust from its suspended station. Down came Stardust getting bigger and bigger, louder and louder. Down came Stardust with a crash!

Dust shot away! Hoofs and hide contracted, seemed buried in the earth, and then bounced with a geyser of wheels, cogs, tubes, rheostats and useless condensers. Up went the electronic shower, down came distended rods and shattered bric-a-brac, mingled with spattering, twisted pieces of torn hide.

Stillness came. A radar eye rolled pathetically to Gadget's feet and lay there, teetering, looking at him accusatively. The dust settled, slowly, quietly, and much of it upon a cowering Miss Franklin whose disarrayed nerves were almost as damaged as the late and unlamented automagic horse.

"Gravity repulsor," said Gadget O'Dowd. "Installed it at the last minute in a streak of proud genius. Works fine, doesn't it, Angus?" He looked benignly at Miss Franklin. "Gravity repulsor, installed to conduct a scientific experiment in the interests of the future safety of stuntmen. Solder seems to have broken so that I couldn't slow it down."

"What . . . what happened?" said Miss Franklin.

"Why," said Gadget, "in the interest of picture research, we installed a gravity repulsor which lifted Stardust out of the trailer and deposited her back here where she belongs. And I think you will find that this experiment cost exactly twenty-five hundred and twenty dollars to conduct, including the cost of the gravity repulsor unit, of course." He looked brightly at the scattered remains which were strewn widely across the flower beds.

Miss Franklin gulped, looked at Gadget with baffled but dawning respect and then took her tired way into her office.

"Loddie," said Angus, "'tis a great project on which we're embarked. But I'm thinkin' if ye keep this up ye'll find it *necessary* to go to the moon—aye, and a divil of a lot farther before we're done."

"Boss," said the worshipful Tony, "that sure was a bang-up solution to dat problem!"

Gadget reached into his jacket pocket and brought out the purchase checks which Mr. Neary had given him for the sale of Stardust. He handed them to Tony. "This hurts me more than I can say, but one must be honest after all. Take them over to Mr. Neary and tell him how sorry we are that his new horse ran away. Tell him it was a bad habit she had anyway."

"Give him back fifty G's?" gaped Tony.

"My boy," said Gadget, "you have evidently forgotten how much money we made off him on the bets. My conscience," he added, with a bright, self-denying smile, "wouldn't permit me to keep his checks for a horse he never owned."

"Your conscience," said Tony, with disgust, "is the most expensive thing we got!" He pulled on his gloves, took the money and drove away.

In the dark of night another mile of tunnel to a "gamma room" was started into the Hollywood Hills. And enough metal for a spaceship's bow was smuggled, the very next day, straight under the vigilant nose of Miss Franklin.

Gadget and Angus and Tony were that much closer to the moon. "I hope humanity appreciates the trouble we've gone to for it," said Gadget. But there was so much noise around the busy forge that Angus and Tony didn't even hear him.

STORY PREVIEW

STORY PREVIEW

NOW that you've just ventured through some of the captivating tales in the Stories from the Golden Age collection by L. Ron Hubbard, turn the page and enjoy a preview of *Beyond All Weapons*. Join Firstin Guide and a handful of colonists who escape from the long reach of a tyrannical Earth government imposing its will on their Martian habitat. They escape on a starship and flee to a new planet to engineer their revenge—yet they do not take into account the irrefutable passage of time.

BEYOND ALL WEAPONS

THE revolt was over and the firing parties had begun. In a single day in Under Washington, three thousand rebels were executed and twelve thousand more condemned to life imprisonment in the camps. And the *Bellerophon* hung fifteen thousand miles out of reach, caught between death by starvation and swifter death by surrender.

She was the last of the rebel ships, the *Bellerophon*. Sent by Admiral Correlli during the last hours of the action to the relief of an isolated community on Mars, she had escaped the debacle which had overtaken all her sister ships in contest with Earth.

The revolt was ill begun and worse ended. But the cause had been bright and the emergency large, and Mars, long-suffering colony of an arbitrary and aged Earth, had at last, as the dying bulldog seeks to take one final grip on the throat of his foe, revolted against Mother Earth.

But there was little sense in recounting those woes now, as Captain Guide well knew. The taxes and embargoes had all but murdered Mars before the revolt had begun. The savage bombardment of the combined navies of Earth had left an expanse of wasted tillage and shattered towns and the colonists had been all but annihilated.

Like her sisters, the *Bellerophon* was a converted merchantman. Any resemblance she bore to a naval spaceship was resident only in the minds of her officers and crew. Plying her trade from Cap City to Denverchicago, she had suffered much from being colonial-built. The inspectors on Earth had inspected her twice as often as regulations demanded and found ten times as much fault. And because she was colonial, her duties, enforced by irksome searches and even crew seizures for the Earth Navy, had all but bankrupted Smiley Smith and the line's directors—not that that mattered now, for the company and all its people were dead in the wreck which had been the finest city in the colonies.

"*I* won't surrender!" said Georges Micard, first mate. "Not while I've got a gun to fire! It's their holiday. Let's give them a few blazing cities to celebrate by!"

Guide, cool, austere, had looked at his mate in silence for a while. He said, "Your plan is not without merit, Georges. We have suffered beyond endurance and our comrades have died gallantly. And a few blazing cities would be much in order were it not for one thing: the barrier."

Georges, optimistic, very young, was apt to forget practical details. The reason Earth had won had been the barrier. So well had the secret been kept that when the colonial fleet had attacked, every missile they had launched at the queen cities of their mother planet had exploded a thousand miles out from target. There was an invisible barrier there, a screen, an electronic ceiling. And Mars, new-formed, braver than she was sensible, had found herself unable to retaliate for the thunder of missiles which had wrenched her cities from their foundations and laid them into dust.

"All right," said Georges, glancing around the wardroom at the other officers. "We'll sit up here until the cruisers come get us and then we'll vanish in a puff of atoms."

"They won't come," said Carteret. "They know we are here, but they'll wait for us to starve. They have every spaceport on Mars and Venus. We're done."

Gloom deepened in the room. Then Albert Firth, their political adviser, an intense-eyed Scot, honed keen in the chill clime of New Iceland, Mars, leaned forward.

"You interested me, Captain, when you spoke today of the drives for which our fleet should have waited. Exactly what were those drives, sir?"

Guide looked at him with understanding. It was time to speak. These people had depleted their own stores of ideas. Hundreds of thousands of colonists were dead, and as fast as the orders for execution could be issued, thousands more were dying. These men would not cavil at thin chances.

"I have had, for some time, a plan," he said.

Eyes whipped to him. They knew Guide. Bilged out of the Space Academy at fourteen for one too many duels, raised by the lawless camps of the southern cap on Mars, cast off by his family, but infinitely esteemed by his comrades and former employers, Firstin Guide was a man to whom one paid attention.

"I think they ought to be whipped," he said quietly.

In more optimistic times, that had been a common opinion

109

on Mars. Since the triarchy of the Polar State had destroyed all free government, the thoughts of less disciplined peoples had run in that vein. Martian colonists were, more lately, refugees from the insensate cruelties and caprices of the Polar regime. And they had all thought that the "snow devils"—that strange race who had managed to adapt their metabolism to the blood-chilling climate of the North Pole, and who in half a century had made their unexploited realm the prime power of Earth—ought to be whipped. But here, in a ship almost out of food, low on ammunition, with half her fuel gone and her cause already lost, those words drew a quick intake of breath from all. But they knew Firstin Guide. He would not speak idly.

To find out more about *Beyond All Weapons* and how you can obtain your copy, go to www.goldenagestories.com.

GLOSSARY

GLOSSARY

STORIES FROM THE GOLDEN AGE *reflect the words and expressions used in the 1930s and 1940s, adding unique flavor and authenticity to the tales. While a character's speech may often reflect regional origins, it also can convey attitudes common in the day. So that readers can better grasp such cultural and historical terms, uncommon words or expressions of the era, the following glossary has been provided.*

ad astra per aspera: (Latin) to the stars through difficulties.

Aida: the name of a popular Italian opera composed by Giuseppe Verdi and one of the most performed operas in North America.

alpha: the first one; the beginning.

Andes: a mountain range that extends the length of the western coast of South America.

arquebuses: heavy portable guns with a trigger mechanism that ignites the powder with a slow-burning fuse. They were invented during the fifteenth century.

astrography: the art of describing or delineating the stars; a description or mapping of the heavens.

batteries: groups of large-caliber weapons used for combined action.

Bell Telephone: the original Bell Telephone Company was founded in 1878 by Alexander Graham Bell's father-in-law. It later merged with other companies to eventually become what is known today as the American Telephone & Telegraph Company (AT&T).

bilged out: failed in one's studies and resigned under compulsion.

bit player: an actor having a very small speaking part in a play, motion picture, etc.

Blarney stone: a stone set in the wall below the battlements of the Blarney Castle, a medieval stronghold in Ireland. It is said to bestow the gift of eloquence, the art of using language well and convincingly, to anyone who kisses it.

blockbuster: a high-explosive bomb designed to demolish buildings over a large area.

bolts: short arrows for use with a crossbow.

boomp girls: Hollywood starlets.

buckjumping: moving in sudden jerks; lurching.

bucko officers: officers of a ship who drive their crew by the power of their fists.

bully-boy: fine; excellent or splendid man.

cakewalked: walked with a high prance with a backward tilt.

champ: to make biting or gnashing movements.

cheerio: (chiefly British) usually used as a farewell.

chewed and hewed: pondered and came to an agreement.

chews: pieces of dried tobacco for chewing.

confederated: brought into an alliance.

cuspidor: a large bowl, often of metal, serving as a receptacle for spit, especially from chewing tobacco, in wide use during the nineteenth and early twentieth centuries.

drifting: making a horizontal passageway or tunnel in a rock layer.

ease her: nautical term used to order the steersman to reduce the amount of steerage during a turn. Usually given as an order as the ship approaches the desired course. The term originated during the days of sailing ships and *her* referred to the rudder.

flips: a class of mixed drinks with egg as a defining feature. The most commonly known flip is eggnog. A basic flip calls for a base spirit, such as brandy or rum, egg, sugar, cream and nutmeg.

furlong: a measure of distance equal to 220 yards.

gamma rays: very penetrating rays emitted by radioactive substances.

Garand rifle: a semiautomatic rifle named after designer John Garand (1888–1974).

geldings: male horses that have been castrated.

Ghost Rider, The: a movie from 1935 about a deputy who cleans up a town with the assistance of a ghost.

G-men: government men; agents of the Federal Bureau of Investigation.

Goldwyn, Samuel: (1879–1974) Hollywood independent motion picture producer who had an instrumental role in the formation of the two largest Hollywood studios, Paramount Pictures and Metro-Goldwyn-Mayer.

high road: the surest or best approach.

Horch phaeton: the make and model of a late 1930s high-performance luxury car manufactured in Germany by the Horch Company. The Horch phaeton was a large open automobile with a folding top, seating five or more passengers. August Horch, one of the pioneering figures of Germany's automotive industry, established a line of cars that was known for elegance, luxury and superlative standards in automotive construction. Production of Horch automobiles ceased when World War II began.

hostlers: people who are employed to tend horses.

Huguenot: French Christians who broke away from the Catholic Church in the seventeenth century. They wore eccentric, richly colored clothes.

ken: (Scottish) know; have knowledge of.

kingpin: a main or large bolt in a central position.

Lamarr, Hedy: (1913–2000) a famous Austrian-born American actress known primarily for her great beauty.

lookout: a problem or concern.

Lost Tribe, The: a movie produced by Columbia Pictures in 1949 as the second installment of the "Jungle Jim" series, a comic-strip adventure. The hero of the story, Jungle Jim, helps to drive off white men's efforts to find and take the riches from a tribe hidden in the African wilds.

manganese steel: steel containing manganese (a hard gray metallic element), an alloy invented by Sir Robert Hadfield in 1882, which increases the depth of hardening in the steel, and improves the strength and toughness. This metal can still be shaped when cold without fracture, and once fully hardened, has unusual shock-resistant properties.

Man o' War: a horse, considered by many to be the greatest US thoroughbred racehorse of all time.

man-o'-war: a warship; combat ship.

meet her: nautical term used to order the steersman to turn in the opposite direction in order to check or stop a ship's swing. The term originated during the days of sailing ships and *her* referred to the rudder.

Moloch: a god to whom children were sacrificed. It was depicted as a man with the head of a bull.

Pitts, ZaSu: (1894–1963) a famous American film actress who appeared in hundreds of movies from 1917 until 1963.

plate: in printing or photography, an image or copy.

quirt: a riding whip with a short handle and a braided leather lash.

RCA: Radio Corporation of America; a privately owned radio broadcasting corporation formed in 1919.

rococo: showy.

rooftree: ridgepole; a long beam of wood that runs along the ridge of a roof, and to which the upper ends of the rafters are attached.

Santa Anita: Santa Anita Park; a thoroughbred race track in California known for offering some of the prominent horse racing events in the United States.

Scheherazade: the female narrator of *The Arabian Nights,* who during one thousand and one adventurous nights saved her life by entertaining her husband, the king, with stories.

scurvy: a disease caused by a deficiency of vitamin C, characterized by bleeding gums and the opening of previously healed wounds.

scut: a worthless contemptible person.

Shantung: a peninsula in east China extending into the Yellow Sea.

skinflint: one who is very reluctant to spend money; a miser.

snagger: something that grabs or seizes.

sorrel: a horse with a reddish-brown coat.

SPCA: Society for the Prevention of Cruelty to Animals.

spur: an angular projection, offshoot or branch extending out beyond or away from a main body.

touts: those who give tips on racehorses, usually with expectation of some personal reward in return.

Westinghouse: George Westinghouse, Jr. (1846–1914), American entrepreneur, engineer and manufacturer who received more than 400 patents for his many inventions including a practical method for transmitting electric power. He founded the Westinghouse Electric Company in 1886.

will-o'-the-wisp: somebody or something that is misleading or elusive.

wrinkle: a clever trick, method or device, especially one that is new and different.

L. Ron Hubbard
in the Golden Age
of Pulp Fiction

In writing an adventure story
a writer has to know that he is adventuring
for a lot of people who cannot.
The writer has to take them here and there
about the globe and show them
excitement and love and realism.
As long as that writer is living the part of an
adventurer when he is hammering
the keys, he is succeeding with his story.

Adventuring is a state of mind.
If you adventure through life, you have a
good chance to be a success on paper.

Adventure doesn't mean globe-trotting,
exactly, and it doesn't mean great deeds.
Adventuring is like art.
You have to live it to make it real.

— *L. RON HUBBARD*

L. Ron Hubbard
and American
Pulp Fiction

B ORN March 13, 1911, L. Ron Hubbard lived a life at least as expansive as the stories with which he enthralled a hundred million readers through a fifty-year career.

Originally hailing from Tilden, Nebraska, he spent his formative years in a classically rugged Montana, replete with the cowpunchers, lawmen and desperadoes who would later people his Wild West adventures. And lest anyone imagine those adventures were drawn from vicarious experience, he was not only breaking broncs at a tender age, he was also among the few whites ever admitted into Blackfoot society as a bona fide blood brother. While if only to round out an otherwise rough and tumble youth, his mother was that rarity of her time—a thoroughly educated woman—who introduced her son to the classics of Occidental literature even before his seventh birthday.

But as any dedicated L. Ron Hubbard reader will attest, his world extended far beyond Montana. In point of fact, and as the son of a United States naval officer, by the age of eighteen he had traveled over a quarter of a million miles. Included therein were three Pacific crossings to a then still mysterious Asia, where he ran with the likes of Her British Majesty's agent-in-place

L. Ron Hubbard, left, at Congressional Airport, Washington, DC, 1931, with members of George Washington University flying club.

for North China, and the last in the line of Royal Magicians from the court of Kublai Khan. For the record, L. Ron Hubbard was also among the first Westerners to gain admittance to forbidden Tibetan monasteries below Manchuria, and his photographs of China's Great Wall long graced American geography texts.

Upon his return to the United States and a hasty completion of his interrupted high school education, the young Ron Hubbard entered George Washington University. There, as fans of his aerial adventures may have heard, he earned his wings as a pioneering barnstormer at the dawn of American aviation. He also earned a place in free-flight record books for the longest sustained flight above Chicago. Moreover, as a roving reporter for *Sportsman Pilot* (featuring his first professionally penned articles), he further helped inspire a generation of pilots who would take America to world airpower.

Immediately beyond his sophomore year, Ron embarked on the first of his famed ethnological expeditions, initially to then untrammeled Caribbean shores (descriptions of which would later fill a whole series of West Indies mystery-thrillers). That the Puerto Rican interior would also figure into the future of Ron Hubbard stories was likewise no accident. For in addition to cultural studies of the island, a 1932–33

LRH expedition is rightly remembered as conducting the first complete mineralogical survey of a Puerto Rico under United States jurisdiction.

There was many another adventure along this vein: As a lifetime member of the famed Explorers Club, L. Ron Hubbard charted North Pacific waters with the first shipboard radio direction finder, and so pioneered a long-range navigation system universally employed until the late twentieth century. While not to put too fine an edge on it, he also held a rare Master Mariner's license to pilot any vessel, of any tonnage in any ocean.

Yet lest we stray too far afield, there is an LRH note at this juncture in his saga, and it reads in part:

"I started out writing for the pulps, writing the best I knew, writing for every mag on the stands, slanting as well as I could."

To which one might add: His earliest submissions date from the summer of 1934, and included tales drawn from true-to-life Asian adventures, with characters roughly modeled on British/American intelligence operatives he had known in Shanghai. His early Westerns were similarly peppered with details drawn from personal experience. Although therein lay a first hard lesson from the often cruel world of the pulps. His first Westerns were soundly rejected as lacking the authenticity of a Max Brand yarn

Capt. L. Ron Hubbard in Ketchikan, Alaska, 1940, on his Alaskan Radio Experimental Expedition, the first of three voyages conducted under the Explorers Club flag.

(a particularly frustrating comment given L. Ron Hubbard's Westerns came straight from his Montana homeland, while Max Brand was a mediocre New York poet named Frederick Schiller Faust, who turned out implausible six-shooter tales from the terrace of an Italian villa).

Nevertheless, and needless to say, L. Ron Hubbard persevered and soon earned a reputation as among the most publishable names in pulp fiction, with a ninety percent placement rate of first-draft manuscripts. He was also among the most prolific, averaging between seventy and a hundred thousand words a month. Hence the rumors that L. Ron Hubbard had redesigned a typewriter for faster keyboard action and pounded out manuscripts on a continuous roll of butcher paper to save the precious seconds it took to insert a single sheet of paper into manual typewriters of the day.

That all L. Ron Hubbard stories did not run beneath said byline is yet another aspect of pulp fiction lore. That is, as publishers periodically rejected manuscripts from top-drawer authors if only to avoid paying top dollar, L. Ron Hubbard and company just as frequently replied with submissions under various pseudonyms. In Ron's case, the

A MAN OF MANY NAMES

Between 1934 and 1950, L. Ron Hubbard authored more than fifteen million words of fiction in more than two hundred classic publications. To supply his fans and editors with stories across an array of genres and pulp titles, he adopted fifteen pseudonyms in addition to his already renowned L. Ron Hubbard byline.

Winchester Remington Colt
Lt. Jonathan Daly
Capt. Charles Gordon
Capt. L. Ron Hubbard
Bernard Hubbel
Michael Keith
Rene Lafayette
Legionnaire 148
Legionnaire 14830
Ken Martin
Scott Morgan
Lt. Scott Morgan
Kurt von Rachen
Barry Randolph
Capt. Humbert Reynolds

126

list included: Rene Lafayette, Captain Charles Gordon, Lt. Scott Morgan and the notorious Kurt von Rachen—supposedly on the lam for a murder rap, while hammering out two-fisted prose in Argentina. The point: While L. Ron Hubbard as Ken Martin spun stories of Southeast Asian intrigue, LRH as Barry Randolph authored tales of

L. Ron Hubbard, circa 1930, at the outset of a literary career that would finally span half a century.

romance on the Western range—which, stretching between a dozen genres is how he came to stand among the two hundred elite authors providing close to a million tales through the glory days of American Pulp Fiction.

In evidence of exactly that, by 1936 L. Ron Hubbard was literally leading pulp fiction's elite as president of New York's American Fiction Guild. Members included a veritable pulp hall of fame: Lester "Doc Savage" Dent, Walter "The Shadow" Gibson, and the legendary Dashiell Hammett—to cite but a few.

Also in evidence of just where L. Ron Hubbard stood within his first two years on the American pulp circuit: By the spring of 1937, he was ensconced in Hollywood, adopting a Caribbean thriller for Columbia Pictures, remembered today as *The Secret of Treasure Island*. Comprising fifteen thirty-minute episodes, the L. Ron Hubbard screenplay led to the most profitable matinée serial in Hollywood history. In accord with Hollywood culture, he was thereafter continually called upon

The 1937 Secret of Treasure Island, *a fifteen-episode serial adapted for the screen by L. Ron Hubbard from his novel,* Murder at Pirate Castle.

to rewrite/doctor scripts—most famously for long-time friend and fellow adventurer Clark Gable.

In the interim—and herein lies another distinctive chapter of the L. Ron Hubbard story—he continually worked to open Pulp Kingdom gates to up-and-coming authors. Or, for that matter, anyone who wished to write. It was a fairly unconventional stance, as markets were already thin and competition razor sharp. But the fact remains, it was an L. Ron Hubbard hallmark that he vehemently lobbied on behalf of young authors—regularly supplying instructional articles to trade journals, guest-lecturing to short story classes at George Washington University and Harvard, and even founding his own creative writing competition. It was established in 1940, dubbed the Golden Pen, and guaranteed winners both New York representation and publication in *Argosy*.

But it was John W. Campbell Jr.'s *Astounding Science Fiction* that finally proved the most memorable LRH vehicle. While every fan of L. Ron Hubbard's galactic epics undoubtedly knows the story, it nonetheless bears repeating: By late 1938, the pulp publishing magnate of Street & Smith was determined to revamp *Astounding Science Fiction* for broader readership. In particular, senior editorial director F. Orlin Tremaine called for stories with a stronger *human element*. When acting editor John W. Campbell balked, preferring his spaceship-driven tales, Tremaine enlisted Hubbard. Hubbard, in turn, replied with the genre's first truly *character-driven* works, wherein heroes are pitted not against bug-eyed monsters but the mystery and majesty of deep space itself—and thus was launched the Golden Age of Science Fiction.

The names alone are enough to quicken the pulse of any science fiction aficionado, including LRH friend and protégé, Robert Heinlein, Isaac Asimov, A. E. van Vogt and Ray Bradbury. Moreover, when coupled with LRH stories of fantasy, we further come to what's rightly been described as the foundation of every modern tale of horror: L. Ron Hubbard's immortal *Fear.* It was rightly proclaimed by Stephen King as one of the very few works to genuinely warrant that overworked term "classic"—as in: *"This is a classic tale of creeping, surreal menace and horror. . . . This is one of the really, really good ones."*

L. Ron Hubbard, 1948, among fellow science fiction luminaries at the World Science Fiction Convention in Toronto.

To accommodate the greater body of L. Ron Hubbard fantasies, Street & Smith inaugurated *Unknown*—a classic pulp if there ever was one, and wherein readers were soon thrilling to the likes of *Typewriter in the Sky* and *Slaves of Sleep* of which Frederik Pohl would declare: *"There are bits and pieces from Ron's work that became part of the language in ways that very few other writers managed."*

And, indeed, at J. W. Campbell Jr.'s insistence, Ron was regularly drawing on themes from the Arabian Nights and so introducing readers to a world of genies, jinn, Aladdin and Sinbad—all of which, of course, continue to float through cultural mythology to this day.

At least as influential in terms of post-apocalypse stories was L. Ron Hubbard's 1940 *Final Blackout.* Generally acclaimed as the finest anti-war novel of the decade and among the ten best works of the genre ever authored—here, too, was a tale that would live on in ways few other writers imagined.

Hence, the later Robert Heinlein verdict: "Final Blackout *is as perfect a piece of science fiction as has ever been written.*"

Like many another who both lived and wrote American pulp adventure, the war proved a tragic end to Ron's sojourn in the pulps. He served with distinction in four theaters and was highly decorated for commanding corvettes in the North Pacific. He was also grievously wounded in combat, lost many a close friend and colleague and thus resolved to say farewell to pulp fiction and devote himself to what it had supported these many years—namely, his serious research.

Portland, Oregon, 1943; L. Ron Hubbard, captain of the US Navy subchaser PC 815.

But in no way was the LRH literary saga at an end, for as he wrote some thirty years later, in 1980:

"Recently there came a period when I had little to do. This was novel in a life so crammed with busy years, and I decided to amuse myself by writing a novel that was pure *science fiction."*

That work was *Battlefield Earth: A Saga of the Year 3000*. It was an immediate *New York Times* bestseller and, in fact, the first international science fiction blockbuster in decades. It was not, however, L. Ron Hubbard's magnum opus, as that distinction is generally reserved for his next and final work: The 1.2 million word *Mission Earth*.

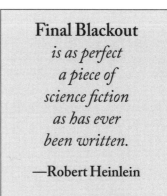

Final Blackout *is as perfect a piece of science fiction as has ever been written.*

—Robert Heinlein

How he managed those 1.2 million words in just over twelve months is yet another piece of the L. Ron Hubbard legend. But the fact remains, he did indeed author a ten-volume *dekalogy* that lives in publishing history for the fact that each and every volume of the series was also a *New York Times* bestseller.

Moreover, as subsequent generations discovered L. Ron Hubbard through republished works and novelizations of his screenplays, the mere fact of his name on a cover signaled an international bestseller. . . . Until, to date, sales of his works exceed hundreds of millions, and he otherwise remains among the most enduring and widely read authors in literary history. Although as a final word on the tales of L. Ron Hubbard, perhaps it's enough to simply reiterate what editors told readers in the glory days of American Pulp Fiction:

He writes the way he does, brothers, because he's been there, seen it and done it!

THE STORIES FROM THE GOLDEN AGE

Your ticket to adventure starts here with the Stories from the Golden Age collection by master storyteller L. Ron Hubbard. These gripping tales are set in a kaleidoscope of exotic locales and brim with fascinating characters, including some of the most vile villains, dangerous dames and brazen heroes you'll ever get to meet.

The entire collection of over one hundred and fifty stories is being released in a series of eighty books and audiobooks. For an up-to-date listing of available titles, go to www.goldenagestories.com.

AIR ADVENTURE

FAR-FLUNG ADVENTURE

SEA ADVENTURE

TALES FROM THE ORIENT

MYSTERY

FANTASY

SCIENCE FICTION

WESTERN

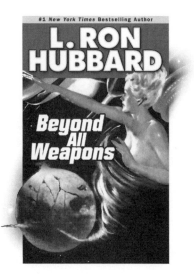

JOIN THE PULP REVIVAL
America in the 1930s and 40s

Pulp fiction was in its heyday and 30 million readers were regularly riveted by the larger-than-life tales of master storyteller L. Ron Hubbard. For this was pulp fiction's golden age, when the writing was raw and every page packed a walloping punch.

That magic can now be yours. An evocative world of nefarious villains, exotic intrigues, courageous heroes and heroines—a world that today's cinema has barely tapped for tales of adventure and swashbucklers.

Enroll today in the Stories from the Golden Age Club and begin receiving your monthly feature edition selected from more than 150 stories in the collection.

You may choose to enjoy them as either a paperback or audiobook for the special membership price of $9.95 each month along with FREE shipping and handling.

CALL TOLL-FREE: 1-877-8GALAXY
(1-877-842-5299) OR GO ONLINE TO
www.goldenagestories.com
AND BECOME PART OF THE PULP REVIVAL!

Prices are set in US dollars only. For non-US residents, please call
1-323-466-7815 for pricing information. Free shipping available for US residents only.

Galaxy Press, 7051 Hollywood Blvd., Suite 200, Hollywood, CA 90028